H. ST. JOHN PHILBY, IBN SAUD AND PALESTINE

by

Jerald L. Thompson
B.S., United States Military Academy, 1971

Fredonia Books
Amsterdam, The Netherlands

H. St. John Philby, IBN Saud and Palestine

by
Jerald L. Thompson

ISBN: 1-58963-842-5

Reprinted from the 1982 edition

Fredonia Books
Amsterdam, The Netherlands
http://www.fredoniabooks.com

ABSTRACT

The purpose of this work was to determine the policy of the
founder of Saudi Arabia, King Ibn Saud, toward the establishment
of a Jewish entity in Palestine - the "Palestine problem." H. St.
John Philby was a British author, explorer and convert to Islam
who had a very close association with Ibn Saud. Studying Philby's
relationship with Ibn Saud and his attempts to get the King to
negotiate with the Zionists provides a clear understanding of the
original Saudi involvement in the Palestine problem.

The approach taken in this study was to first establish the
historical context of St. John Philby (1885-1960) and Ibn Saud
(1880-1953) and then focus on this involvement with the Palestine
problem between 1936-1945. The Palestine study starts with the Arab
revolt of 1936. It then traces the development of Philby's solution
to the problem, its acceptance and advocacy by Zionists to the
British and American governments, and ends with Ibn Saud's discussion
on Palestine with President F. D. Roosevelt in 1945.

Philby's plan to solve the Palestine problem did not reach
fruition because the differences between the Arabs and the Jews were
irreconcilable, and it appears that neither the British or the Americans
really understood the Arab viewpoint. King Ibn Saud was consistently
opposed to the establishment of any Jewish State and until 1945 he
believed that the Great Powers would not violate the Arab trust.

ACKNOWLEDGEMENTS

This thesis was completed only because of the tremendous support I received. I am especially grateful to Professor Rose L. Greaves for her professional guidance and assistance which led me to the subject of this work. My research was substantially aided because of her generosity in granting me access to many of her books and copies of British documents. Her understanding counsel made my progress through this introduction to scholarship much less painful than it might have been. I am indebted to Professor George W. Gawrych for his patience and guidance throughout the construction of this thesis. His efforts are sincerely appreciated. I am also thankful for the encouragement given by Professor Carl Lande.

The research for this thesis was tremendously facilitated by the conscientous efforts of the library staff of the Command and General Staff College. Special thanks are deserved by Mr. Ed Gast for his untiring assistance in obtaining material from other facilities I am also very grateful to Miss Connie Randel for her expert typing of this thesis and for her kind patience and assistance in preparing the final product.

My greatest debt is to my loving wife Eileen and to our children, Jennifer and Eric. Their understanding and love gave me the support I needed to complete this work. I thank God for the blessing He has given me.

TABLE OF CONTENTS

INTRODUCTION

Saudi Arabia is the focal point of the Moslem world because it is both the birthplace of Islam and the site of the two Holy Cities of Mecca and Medina. As the repository of vast quantities of oil, it is also a focal point for the oil consuming nations of the world. Currently Saudi Arabia is attempting to assert a leading role in negotiating the major issue within the Middle East by presenting a comprehensive Arab peace plan for the Arab-Israeli conflict. The significance of this departure from past policies can be appreciated more with an understanding of the relationship between the founder of Saudi Arabia, King Ibn Saud, and the "Palestine problem" which preceded the current conflict.

St. John Philby (1885-1960) was the British author and explorer of Saudi Arabia who had a very close association with Ibn Saud (1880-1953). Studying Philby's relationship with Ibn Saud and his attempts to get the King to negotiate with the Zionists provides a clear understanding of the original Saudi involvement in the Palestine problem.

This study begins with a biographical sketch of the interrelated lives of St. John Philby and Ibn Saud, thereby establishing the historical context for an assessment of their relationship with the Palestine problem. In the second chapter, Philby's efforts to devise a solution will be presented as they relate to the complex interaction between the Arabs, the Zionists, the British and the Americans during the period 1936-1939. The third chapter will trace Philby's "plan" from 1940 to 1945 as he and Dr. Chaim Weizmann, President of the

1

World Zionist Organization, advocated its acceptance by the British and American Governments and by Ibn Saud. The conclusion will address the contributing factors which precluded the acceptance of Philby's plan.

The majors sources used in this study are:

1) Philby's papers from St. Anthony's, Oxford; his book on Ibn Saud, _Arabian Jubilee_ (1953) and Elizabeth Monroe's biography, _Philby of Arabia_ (1973).

2) Ibn Saud's public statements in interviews conducted by Philby and an editor from _Life_ magazine.

3) Letters and messages between Ibn Saud and President F. D. Roosevelt that were published by the United States State Department in the Foreign Relations of the United States series (herein refered to as F.R.U.S. with the appropriate years and volume added).

4) Dr. Chaim Weizmann's autobiography, _Trial and Error_ (1949), and a letter obtained from the Zionist Archives in Jerusalem.

5) Official British reports, letters, messages and attached minutes prepared by the Foreign Office (F.O.); the Colonial Office (C.O.); and Ministers and Officers in the Middle East and India. These documents were obtained from the British Public Record Office (P.R.O.) and Command Paper (Cmd).

Some of the most significant documents have been reproduced and are included in the appendicies.

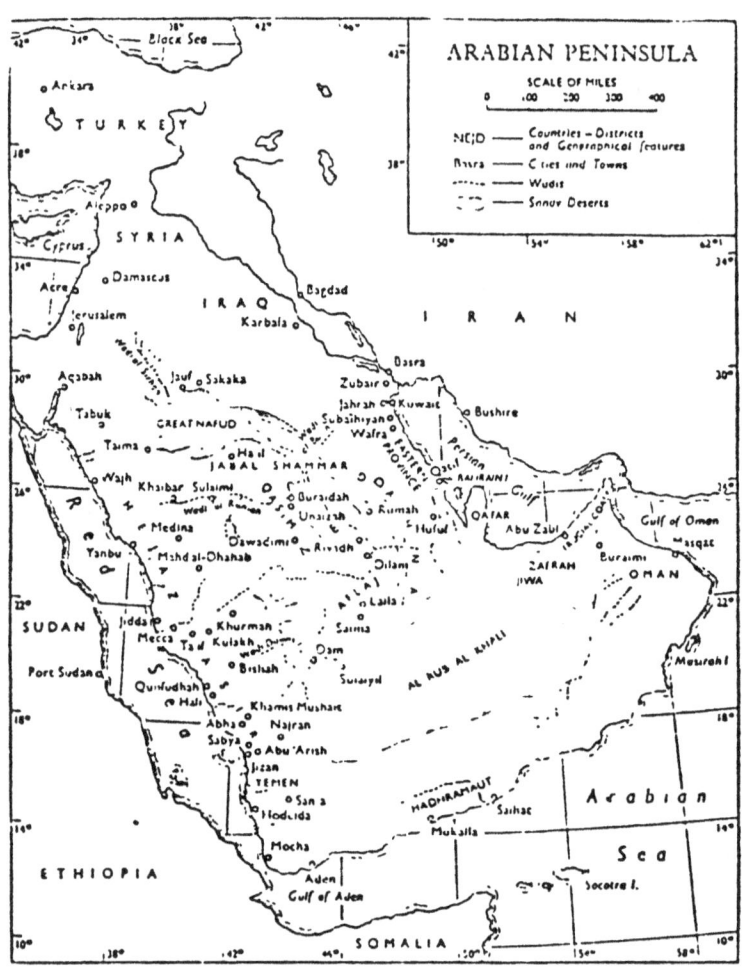

Figure 1: Arabian Peninsula

Source: Winder, R. Bayly. <u>Saudi Arabia in the Nineteenth Century,</u>
New York: St. Martin's Press, 1965.

CHAPTER ONE

THE INTERRELATED LIVES OF ST. JOHN PHILBY AND IBN SAUD

This chapter will present biographical sketches of the Englishman St. John Philby and his Arab hero Ibn Saud. The purpose is to
provide sufficient information to enable the reader to develop an
appreciation of the two characters and their relative importance in
the history of the Middle East.

Philby's Pre-Arabian Days (1885-1917)

Harry St. John Bridges Philby was born on April 3, 1885, in
Ceylon. His father Henry M. Philby was trying to be a tea planter.
His mother, May, was trying to endure Henry; but after bearing four
children and innumerable heartaches, she left Ceylon to raise her
children in England.

St. John Philby demonstrated a keen intellect as a young student
and won a scholarship to Westminster. A scholarship was the only way
he could have obtained a higher education owing to the financial
problems of his mother. At the age of 13, St. John Philby became a
Queen's scholar and did exceptionally well. He was elected Captain
of his class during his senior year in 1903. In accordance with the
school's tradition, his successor wrote a review of Philby's
tenure in which Philby was accredited with raising the moral
standards of conduct, order and general discipline but was criticized
as being autocratic -- and not knowing how to conceal his iron hand
in a velvet glove. Tact would never be one of his strong points.

Philby studied modern languages at Trinity College, Cambridge,
from 1904 to 1907. He took his vacations in Europe to practice his

French and German. He was accepted for the Indian Civil Service and spent an additional year at Cambridge in officer training and learning Persian and Urdu.[2]

In December 1908, St. John Philby arrived in India. While enroute to his first Civil Service post in Lahore a train accident nearly terminated his career. His diligence and ability to work with the people impressed his superiors. The pay for a junior civil service officer was only £30 a month, but Philby's cost of living in the Punjab was very little. He paid £1 for rent and £4 for food and was then able to send the majority of his pay to his mother. He found that developing proficiency in languages earned him bonuses and therefore he spent a good deal of effort picking up dialects of Urdu and Baluch.[3]

While on a leave to Rawalpindi, he met a beautiful young lady, Dora Johnson, the daughter of an officer of the Indian Public Works Department. Philby's superiors counseled him; stating that the general policy was that junior officers should not be married until they had at least four years in service. His mother was apprehensive about a loss of her allowance and thus opposed his marriage. Disregarding the opposition, Philby married Dora on September 20, 1910.[4] During the next year his mother was not able to manage financially and Philby had her move to India. Kim Philby was born on New Year's Day, 1912.

As World War I developed, Philby resented being in a distant outpost. His brother, Paddy, was killed in 1914, two days after entering the trenches in France. Philby tried every means possible to get where the action was, but to no avail. In February 1915, he

went to Calcutta to take an honors examination in Urdu. Upon
passing the exam, he received a promotion to become the head of the
Language Board. With the position came a doubling of his pay. He
had to move to Calcutta, but Dora would not join him. She could not
take the environment there and stayed in Rawalpindi.[5] He did not
have to endure Calcutta long. British advances in Mesopotamia against
the Turks were such that Sir Percy Cox, the political officer in
charge of occupied territory, was short of linguists and administrators
Cox cabled to India for more linguists. St. John Philby was transferred to Mesopotamia.

In November 1915, Philby sailed for Basra. When he arrived Sir
Percy Cox gave him a tough mission. He was to study the finances
of the occupied territory and draw up a regular system of civil
accounts. Since this was his best line of work he was delighted.[6]
The Turkish administrators had taken all of their records with them
and the Indian civil servants who had preceeded Philby had tried to
impose the Indian system on the Arabs. Philby studied the situation
in detail and then devised a system appropriate for local conditions.
He also set up a tax and banking system using promissary notes which
greatly reduced the burdensome problem of gold flow with England.
Sir Percy Cox was greatly impressed but Philby's peers were dis-
gruntled. He was hard to work with and would be high-handed in order
to achieve his ends.[7]

By 1917 Philby was made a district officer in Amarra. Dora
joined him for two months but then returned to India when Philby
was transferred to Baghdad to be Sir Percy's secretary. While acting
as secretary to Sir Percy, Philby tended to impose his thinking on

the functioning of various district offices. Arnold Wilson was the District Officer in Basra and in October he complained to Sir Percy about Philby's interference in his operations. As fate would have it, at this time Sir Percy needed to send a liaison officer to Ibn Saud. The British wanted Ibn Saud to stop the smuggling of supplies to the Turks in Syria that were passing through the Shammar region from Kuwait.[8] Philby wanted to be the liaison officer to Ibn Saud and Wilson wanted to be Sir Percy's secretary.[9] St. John Philby was soon enroute to meet the man who would become his hero.

The Emergence of the House of Saud

The Arab leader Abdul-Aziz ibn Abdul-Rahman ibn Faisal Al Sa'ud, known as Ibn Saud, was the man who through the force of his character and religious commitment established the Kingdom of Saudi Arabia. In order to understand how Ibn Saud accomplished this, it is necessary to review the history of the region in terms of the dominant forces. These forces were the major tribes, the Ottomans, the British, and Islam. One can not simply focus on Ibn Saud, but must view his efforts in conjunction with the role of the Wahhabi form of Sunni Islam. For that reason the first step is to review the advent of Muhammed ibn Abd al Wahhab and his relationship with the House of Saud.

Muhammed ibn Abd al Wahhab was born in Uyaynah in the Banu Sinan tribe in 1703. His family was very religious; his father was an expert in Islamic law and was a judge in Uyaynah. Wahhab was a precocious child. He memorized the Koran by the age of ten. His study of Islam took him to the theological centers in Medina,

Damascus, and Basra. Wahhab developed an interpretation of Islam which was drawn from the strict Hanbali scholar Taki al Din Ahmed ibn Taimiya.[10]

The Sunni sect of Islam has four schools of thought in the interpretation of the Koran and the Hadiths - the Hanbali, Shafii, Maliki, and Hanafi in decending order of conservatism. The founder of the Hanbali school was Ahmed ibn Muhammed ibn Hanbal (d. 855).[11] His was a strict view of the Koran as divine law and not in any way a creation of this earth. He therefore limited the principle of 'Kiyas', or reasoning by analogy. Taimiya's interpretation was even more severe in its literalness of interpretation. Wahhab based his religious teachings on the strictes interpretation of the Koran and the Hadiths.

The society in which Wahhab existed did not share his beliefs. There were many variations in religious practice. Some Muslims had reverted to pre-Islamic practices, combining them with Islam. There was tree and stone worship and there were some mystics.[12] Wahhab began to preach a return to the orthodox practices of Muhammad's day, and expecially condemned any form of worship that detracted from the oneness of God. He was expelled from Basra for his extreme teachings and he returned home to Uyaynah. The Bani Khalid tribe, who were Shiites, did not appreciate his teachings either and forced him to leave his village in 1744. He moved his family to Dariyah (12 km northwest of Riyadh) which was ruled by Muhammed ibn Saud.[13]

Muhammed ibn Saud was Shaykh of a small emirate which his family had established in the early 17th century. He welcomed

Wahhab and they soon became allies. They concluded a pact stating that Muhammed ibn Saud would fight for and propagate Wahhabi doctrine in a jihad (holy war), to purify and conquer Arabia. To cement this relationship, Muhammed ibn Saud married Wahhab's daughter.[14]

When Muhammed ibn Saud died in 1765 most of the Najd followed Wahhab's teaching. Abd al Aziz succeeded his father and continued the jihad, taking Riyadh in 1773. The Bani Khalid in al Hasa were defeated by 1792. Wahhab died in 1792, but the force of his teachings continued and the Wahhabi movement spread throughout Arabia.

In 1801 the Wahhabis raided Karbala, a Shiite holy city (approximately 100 km southwest of Baghdad), and sacked the tomb of Hussein ibn Ali, the prophet's grandson. On April 3, 1801 Mecca was taken and the Wahhabis destroyed all symbols of idolatry and anything else that violated the precepts of Islam as taught by Wahhab. Shiites assassinated Abd al Aziz in November, 1803, in revenge for the 1801 attack on Karbala.[15] His son Saud succeeded him, and, by April 1804 he took Medina. The expansion into the Hijaz (west coast area) brought the Saudis into direct conflict with the Ottomans. The Saudis had allowed Sharif Ghalib to continue administering the Hijaz area, but the Pasha in Baghdad had suffered a loss of prestige and income when they took the holy cities. The Ottoman Sultan in Constantinople asked his viceroy in Egypt, Muhammed Ali, to attack the Saudis and return the area to Ottoman control. In 1811, Muhammed Ali's son Tusan led expeditions against the Saudi and found them to be very able fighters. Mecca was recaptured by January 1813. Muhammed Ali took personal control of the fighting in 1813.[16] Saud died in 1814 and his son, Abd Allah became his

successor. Muhammed Ali returned to Egypt in 1815 to address problems
concerning his governorship. His son, Ibrahim, returned to press
the Saudis in 1816. Abd Allah retreated to Dariya where he was
captured, and the city was razed. In 1818 Muhammed Ali sent Abd
Allah to Constantinople where he was beheaded.[17] Thus the first
Saudi dynasty came to an end.

After the destruction of Dariyah, Turki ibn Abd Allah, Abd
Allah's uncle, moved the Saudi clan to Riyadh. He organized troops
to joust the Egyptians and extended his control over all of the Najd,
al Hasa, and south to the Buriami Oasis in Oman. A rival within the
family assissinated Turki in 1834. Turki's son, Faisal, killed the
assassin and became the ruler.[18] Muhammed Ali, in an attempt to
expand his influence within the Ottoman Empire, decided to bring
Arabia into his sphere and brought forth a rival claimant to lead
the Saudi. Khalid ibn Saud, Faisal's cousin had been in an Egyptian
prison since 1816. In 1838, Muhammed Ali made Khalid the Egyptian
vassal in Riyadh, while Faisal was made a prisoner in Cairo. Muhammed
Ali's control extended over the Najd and al Hasa until 1840 when
the British rebuffed his expansion toward Yemen, forcing him to withdraw from Arabia. Khalid continued in control until replaced by
Abdullah II. Faisal escaped from Egypt in 1843, and resumed his
position as leader until his death in 1865.[19]

The next twenty-four years were marked by a power struggle
between Faisal's two sons, Abdullah III and Saud. Abdullah III
ruled from 1865 to 1871 and then from 1875 until his death in
1889. Saud ruled from 1871 until his death in 1875. Feuds within
the Saudi family allowed the Ottomans to repossess the Hejaz (in

1884); Munammea ibn Rashid, in Hail, took this opportunity to increase his influence over the tribes in the northern province of Jabal Shammar. Abd al Rahman succeeded his brother, Abdullah III in 1889 but was soon under pressure from Ibn Rashid. In 1891 Ibn Rashid forced Abd al Rahman to leave Riyadh with his family, and they eventually found refuge in Kuwait.[20] Abd al Aziz II, his son, was then eleven years old.

Abdul-Aziz ibn Abdul-Rahman ibn Faisal Al Sa'ud (Ibn Saud) spent his time in Kuwait learning the Koran, horsemanship, and the ways of war. Mubarak, the ruler of Kuwait, was an enemy of Ibn Rashid and thus was willing to support a Saudi move against him. In 1901, Ibn Saud engaged the Rashidis in battle at Sarif but was repulsed. However, in 1902, with a force of approximately 40 men, he conducted a dawn raid into Riyadh and recaptured it.[21] His father abdicated the secular title of Amir (Chieftain) to his son, but retained the title of Imam (after the death of Wahhab, the religious leadership position was, through marriage ties, kept within the Saud family lineage). Ibn Saud led his forces against the Rashidis and by 1906 re-established Saudi rule in the Najd. His expansion was held in check when one of his brothers, Sa'd, was held hostage by Hussein, a Hashemite who had been installed as Sharif of Mecca by the Ottomans in 1908. (Sharif was the Ottoman title for the governor of Mecca, who was a descendant of the Prophet Muhammed through his daughter Fatima.) When his brother was released, Saudi forces quickly eliminated the Turks in al-Hasa and established Saudi control of the region by 1913.

As Ibn Saud expanded his territory he needed additional forces to maintain his control. He was an ardent believer of the Wahhabi precepts and revived the movement by mobilizing the Ikhwan al Muslimin (Muslim Brethren). Agricultural oasis settlements (hijra) were formed throughout the Najd with Ikhwan at each one. The purpose was to breakdown tribal allegiances, inculcate Wahhabism, and provide ready reserves. By 1912 there were 11,000 Ikhwan al Muslimin.[22]

During World War I Ibn Saud was a minor peripheral power in the eyes of the British government. The British gave him very limited aid to pursue his battles with Ibn Rashid. A treaty with Britain was negotiated in December 1915 which recognized Ibn Saud as Amir of the Najd and al Hasa.[23] Ibn Saud in turn was to continue fighting the Rashidis, thereby blocking the smuggling of supplies to the Turks through Kuwait. The British tried to convince Ibn Saud to participate in a coordinated Arab revolt against the Ottomans, but he would have had to be subordinate to Sharif Hussein, and that was unthinkable.[24] Also, Ibn Saud's forces were not adquately armed nor were they provisioned for such an offensive. So in 1916 Hussein and his British advisor, T.E. Lawrence, commenced their attacks on the Ottomans in the Hejaz, while Ibn Saud tried to build up his forces. In November 1917, Sir Percy Cox dispatched St. John Philby to be a liaison officer to Ibn Saud.[25]

Philby and Ibn Saud (1917-1919)

Traveling by camel, St. John Philby arrived in Riyadh on November 30, 1917; his mission was three-fold. The first priority was to have Ibn Saud conduct a campaign against the Turks' ally Ibn

Rashid in Hail. Secondly, Philby was to convince Ibn Saud that he should improve his relations with his eastern neighbors adjacent to and in Kuwait. The intent was to improve the blockade of supplies to Turkish forces via caravans from the Persian Gulf. Finally, Philby was to try to facilitate an easing of tension between Ibn Saud and Sharif Hussein in the Hijaz.[26]

To accomplish the first task Ibn Saud listed his requirements. He had the men but would need field guns; 10,000 rifles with ammunitition; £20,000 (gold) for food and transport; and £50,000 per month to pay 10,000 men. He expected the campaign to take three months. Philby agreed to convey these requirements to Baghdad. Ibn Saud also agreed to improve his ties with the tribes in the east. However, he had doubts about the effectiveness of a blockade because business with the Turks in the north was a lucrative proposition for desert traders.

Philby found that his third task was the most difficult. Ibn Saud and Sharif Hussein were antagonists. Also, Ibn Saud was irked that his stipend was only £5,000 per month while Hussein received £200,000 a month.[27] (Hussein and T.E. Lawrence were achieving more results by forcing the Turks to withdraw from the Hijaz, whereas Ibn Saud was not contributing as much to the British effort). Philby talked Ibn Saud into allowing him to travel across to Jidda with the intention of returning via the same route with Dr. Ronald Storrs, then Oriental Secretary to the High Commissioner in Egypt. This exercise would prove that Ibn Saud controlled the vast desert and could protect British officials (Hussein depicted Ibn Saud as too weak to do this); and it would allow Ibn Saud direct contact with a high official to whom he could present his request for more

support. On December 9th, Philby proceeded on to Jidda, traversing

the 450 miles without incident in fifteen days.[28] As he travelled

he mapped the route and collected soil samples. This would be his

practice whenever he travelled in Arabia.

His arrival was not expected and Sharif Hussein was very

displeased. Hussein had been embarassed by Philby's trip, as it was

evidence of Ibn Saud's control of the desert. The local British

officer reported Philby's arrival to Cairo and Commander D.G. Hogarth

of the Arab Bureau was sent to help work out an agreement with

Hussein. On 6 January 1918, Hogarth met Philby and the two men

proceeded to talk with Sharif Hussein. When Philby spoke of Ibn

Saud, Hussein lost his composure and proceeded to expound upon the

threat that the Wahhabi movement posed to his territory. Philby

failed to remain tactful and the two soon became irritated with one

another and had an argument.[29] Having failed to achieve his objective

in Jidda, Philby wanted to return to Riyadh the way he had come.

Hussein refused, and on 14 January Philby had to return with Hogarth

on a cruiser to Cairo. In Cairo Philby was the toast of the officer's

club and the intelligence section, where the stories of his trip

across Arabia were met with great interest. Hogarth, in an effort

to broaden Philby's perspective of the overall British effort, took

him to visit Allenby's headquarters in Jerusalem. Philby started

looking at the prospects of a better job for himself in Syria as

Allenby advanced, for he was not yet totally committed to Ibn Saud.

Philby returned to Riyadh via Bombay where he had a few days

with his wife. Once back in Riyadh, he continued to press Ibn Saud to attack Ibn Rashid in Hail and presented him with the necessary £20,000. The number of rifles to be issued had been reduced to 1,000. Ibn Saud did not want his people to believe that he was being supervised by the British, so he told Philby to depart from Riyadh while preparations for the attack were being made. This suited Philby because he wanted to explore the region south of Riyadh. On the 5th of May he started his mapping expedition, which would extend to Suliyil and cover over 600 miles before his return on the 24th of June.[30]

Philby continually recorded his observations on the region's topography, demography, and people while at the same time gathering samples of soil and fossils. All of his experiences in Arabia up to this point are recorded in great detail in his two volume work, The Heart of Arabia (1922). The books are fairly readable. They are a combination of a travel-log, diary, and scientific notebook. Professor Newton of the British Museum wrote in his report summary, "We must congratulate Mr. Philby on his explorations, his palaeontological specimens having materially increased our knowledge of the geological structure of this hitherto unknown region of central Arabia."[31] Philby does not consider himself to be an historian in this work. He is simply offering a record of his travels and explorations with the hope that it will be of use.

After returning from his southern exploration, Philby observed Ibn Saud's final preparations for his attack on Hail and Ibn Rashid. After what he felt were endless delays, the Army was finally assembled and Ibn Saud began his campaign. As they progressed north, Philby was required to wait near Anaiza, for Ibn Saud could not afford to lose his liaison with the British. His first liaison officer, Captain Shakespear, had been killed while accompanying him on a foray in January, 1915.[32] "The first attack on Hail in September, 1918, was a failure if not a fiasco, but it represented Ibn Saud's commitment to a policy of imperial expansion."[33] Philby was disappointed at the inconclusive results of the attack. While Philby had been waiting near Anaiza, he was not idle. He roamed the Qasin province and studied the people, their culture, and habitat, and developed genealogical records of Hijaz rulers, one local family, and the house of Saud. When the Army returned to Riyadh, Philby received notice from Baghdad that his mission was terminated. He and Ibn Saud were both very upset and could not understand why support was being taken away when so much was yet to be done. Philby at that time was not aware of Allenby's successful advance on Damascus which meant that the British no longer needed Ibn Saud. Also, Ibn Saud was an opponent of Britain's other ally, King Hussein. The British had recognized Hussein as King of the Hijaz after he turned against the Ottomans. On 4 October, Philby met with Ibn Saud before his departure. Ibn Saud expressed his regard for Philby and told him to convey to the British that he would continue his attack on Ibn Rashid. If the British were willing to support him, fine. If not, he would continue to do what he felt was needed for his people. Ibn Saud had been promised a gift of 1,000 modern rifles, and Philby was to try to get them shipped. Ibn Saud told Philby if he was not successful he could not return.[34] Philby went to Kuwait and was able to convince his superiors of the need to release the rifles. On 18 October, he boarded a steamer to return to Baghdad and then England

Ibn Saud proved true to his word to Philby. By December 1918 he began moving his forces against King Hussein's territory. In May 1919 King Hussein told his son Abdullah to restore order in the Hijaz. On the night of 25-26 May, Abdullah's force was literally "caught sleeping" by the Ikhwan and was wiped out--except for Abdullah who escaped in his night clothes. The memory of this event was indelibly printed on Abdullah's mind. This threat to the Hashimite authority worried the British and Philby was chosen to be an arbitrator. T.E. Lawrence had been the first choice, but he was on leave and not available. The British feared that Ibn Saud was going to make the Pilgrimage to Mecca and then attack Hussein. Philby went to Jidda, but when he arrived his mission was negated. Ibn Saud had declared that he was returning to Riyadh; he would consolidate his gains and prepare for future operations. Philby returned to England to resume his long earned leave and his writing.

In October of 1919 Philby escorted Ibn Saud's son, Prince Amir Faisal, during the latter's visit to England. Faisal's cousin, Ahmed ibn Thunaian, had been commissioned by Ibn Saud to present his desires to the British government. Ibn Saud wanted protection for the Najd's independence and non-interference in its affairs, a British commission to delineate boundaries; removal of the embargo on pilgrims; the granting of a subsidy; and the appointment of Philby as the British political agent in the Najd.[35] The Foreign Office balked and instead recommended negotiations with Hussein. Philby would not return to Arabia just yet.

Philby's Decline in the British Civil Service and Ibn Saud's
Ascendency in Arabia (1920-1925)

Philby enjoyed a notoriety which put him in demand for speaking
engagements; but his reputation also hindered him. In May 1920 he
applied for a goverment position in Palestine and was not accepted.
He had been recommended to Dr. Chaim Weizmann, President of the World
Zionist Organization, who passed his name to Herbert Samuel, the
new High Commissioner. Samuel asked Herbert Young for a second
opinion. Young who had served with Philby in Iraq, stated that
although Philby was a glutton for work and clever, he was also
argumentative and "liable to take a side and stick to it."[36] Based
on this assessment, Samuel rejected Philby; however, events elsewhere
created a demand for his talents.

By July 1920 King Hussein's son Faisal had been ousted from
Damascus by the French; Mustafa Kemal was fighting to establish his
independent Turkey; and rebellion was erupting in Iraq. The British
were concerned about their hold on the region and the security of
their routes to India. Cox picked Philby to be a member of his
staff and they sailed from England at the end of August to go to
Basra. Arnold Wilson had been left in charge in Iraq and his British
officials had directed affairs similar to the way they were conducted
in India. British officers made decisions while Arabs were "advisors."
Cox was determined to turn that relationship around. Philby worked to
identify appropriate Arab officials for the various offices.
Sayyid Talib was selected for the position of Minister of Interior.
Talib was a very ambitious native of Basra who had a reputation for
unscrupulous behavior.[37] Cox had deported him in 1915, but now he

was the best man available. Philby became Talib's advisor. It
was a well paying job and he was able to have Dora join him for what
he thought would be the duration of his career.[38]

The comfortable situation did not last long. At the Cairo
Conference of March 1921 the British determined that the Hashimite
sons of King Hussein were to rule Iraq and Trans-Jordan. Abdullah
was to be a probationary ruler of Transjordan and Faisal would rule
Iraq. When this became known, Talib and Philby fought it. Talib
threatened to lead a rebellion. Faisal was of the Sunni sect of
Islam and Iraq was predominately Shiite. Talib was arrested and
deported to Ceylon and Philby became temporary Minister of Interior.
He did not support Faisal's ascendancy to the throne and Cox had
to release him.[39] Philby took a leave to Persia and returned to
Baghdad in October.

British difficulties in Transjordan provided Philby with another
opportunity to work with an Arab leader and for Arab independence.
Faisal's brother Abdullah had been enthroned in Amman to establish
an Hashimite government within the mandated territory of Palestine.
Transjordan was to be part of the independent territory promised to
the Arabs. Within a few months Abdullah spent his allowance in
largesse to his favorite nomadic tribes. He was pressured by the
French in Syria for providing sanctuary to Syrian rebels who were
using Transjordan as a base for raids into Syria, and by local
tribes out for money. Churchill dispatched T.E. Lawrence to assess
the problem. It was determined that the situation called for a
strong Englishman who knew how to build up an administration, control
spending, and yet support Arab independence. Philby was recommended,

but he had to be interviewed and accepted by Abdullah, T.E. Lawrence, Sir Herbert Samuel (the High Commissioner in Palestine), and finally by Churchill.[40] Philby was assigned as the Chief British Representative to Transjordan in November, 1921.

When Philby accepted his new position, he assumed a very challenging mission which would have to be pursued in an inhospitable environment, and to his and Dora's surprise, at a lower salary. He thrived on the work and got along fairly well with Abdullah, but his wife and babies suffered in the unsanitary conditions of Amman. Dora and the children returned to England in April 1922. Philby participated in a two-month cross-desert railroad survey from Amman through Jauf (north-central Arabia) to Karbala which enraged his British superiors. He had exceeded his authority and negotiated an agreement with the Ruwalla tribe in Jauf to become a part of Transjordan. With Ikhwan advances against Hail and to the north, Philby's superiors worried that his activities in Jauf threatened to pull Britain into a dispute between Abdullah and Ibn Saud.[41] The latter continued his advances north regardless of Philby's activities. As Cox was to soon realize, only British intervention and negotiation would limit Ibn Saud's advances in Arabia.

Ibn Saud took Hail in November 1921 and disposed of the Rashidi threat. He had militarily defeated the Rashidis, whose leader had been assassinated by a cousin the year before.[42] Ibn Saud was very magnanamous to those he defeated. He married the widow of Saud ibn Rashid and adopted her children, thus joining the Saudi and Rashidi houses. This was a technique he would use in the consolidation of his Kingdom.[43] The Ikhwan advances continued north into Iraq and Trans-

Jordan.

The Hashimite rulers were becoming very apprehensive about Ibn Saud's growing power in Arabia, and thus urged Sir Percy Cox to use British bombers to stop the Ikhwan. Bombers were used in March 1922.[44] Cox however did not want to destroy the Anglo-Saudi relations and so he pursued negotiations to settle the border disputes. In April the Treaty of Mohammera was concluded by representatives of Iraq and the Najd. Ibn Saud did not ratify the treaty because it gave tribal areas to Iraq that were claimed by him. Sir Percy Cox and representatives of Iraq and Kuwait met with Ibn Saud at the port of Ugair in late November 1922. Negotiations were extremely difficult but Cox resolved the arguments finally by dictating borders which gave Iraq and Ibn Saud enough territory to placate their demands. Ibn Saud gained the concession of Qoraiyat ul-Milh and the tribal area north of Jauf, while Iraq retained the disputed tribal areas along its border.[45] Cox also established the neutral zones between the Najd and its two neighbors, Iraq and Kuwait. Kuwait, the weakest of the three, lost the greatest amount of territory but was to share equally in any oil found in the neutral zone.[46] Also at this conference, Ibn Saud granted the Anglo-Persian Oil Company the first oil concession on his territory.[47] Peace was restored in Arabia, at least temporarily.

Philby seemed to enjoy a respite from conflict also, but that too was temporary. In October of 1922 he had escorted Abdullah to London. Abdullah was trying to establish the foundation for his eventual assumption of control of the Hijaz and Transjordan after his father passed from the scene. Philby favored the union of the

Hijaz with Transjordan but on the condition that it have a representative system.[48] The only promise Abdullah got from the British was for independence, subject to the mandate, after a peace treaty with Turkey was signed. Abdullah was granted a continuation of his grant-in-aid, additional funds for civil development, and British officers for his Reserve Force (later known as the Arab Legion). During these negotiations Philby had addressed his financial problems to the Colonial Office and had been promised a £200 raise. Philby and Abdullah returned to Amman in January 1923, both thinking that the future was secure.

Philby worked to prepare Transjordan for independence, but in a short while ended up severing his own relationship with the British government. He attempted to establish tourism in Transjordan and thereby provide additional income for Abdullah's government. His excursions to Petra resulted in the expansion of knowledge about the ancient Nabateans, but they did not then generate tourism or expand the royal treasury.[49] Sir Herbert Samuel, the High Commissioner of Palestine and the Mandate, spoke at an Amman celebration of the promised independence but failed to include recognition of Philby's efforts as the British representative. Philby felt snubbed. He had been trying to get Abdullah to curb his tribal ways and establish a representative government, but the leopard's spots were hard to change. He had a serious argument with Abdullah over the destruction of a Byzantine Basilica and Samuel began to bypass him in the conduct of British affairs. The final straw was put on Philby's back in April 1923 when Britain decided to reduce the salaries of Mandate officials. It was determined that the raise Philby was promised in 1922 had not been approved and he had, therefore, been inadvertently overpaying himself as he managed the grant-in-aid funds. Samuel's accounts department in Palestine exchanged heated debates with Philby until they determined he "only" owed £567. On January 24, 1924, Philby submitted his resignation. He had worked hard, endured the privations and frustrations of working in Amman, his family suffered and he was not appreciated by his seniors. Philby left Transjordan in April 1924 to return to England to commence his thirteen months accrued leave and then to terminate his official British service in May 1925.[50]

Just before Philby left Transjordan, events occurred which caused Ibn Saud to resume his fight with the Hashimites. Mustafa Kemal (Ataturk) abolished the Caliphate in Turkey on March 3, 1924. King Hussein claimed the Caliphate on March 5, 1924. Although the Hashimites claimed to be able to trace their ancestry back to the Prophet, most Muslims did not support that claim.[51] Ibn Saud and the Ikhwan became infuriated. In August the Ikhwan attacked Taif and massacred approximately 300 people. Ibn Saud maintained the pressure on the Hijaz, but only in the form of a seige. He did not want the Ikhwan to repeat in Jidda the same fervor they had shown in Taif. King Hussein abdicated to his son Ali and retired to Cyprus.[52]

In the meantime, Philby, who was in England, contemplated working for a seat in Parliament but the Labor Party did not accept him. He wrote articles about the errors and injustice of British Mandate policies in the Middle East. The possibility of an academic post was remote. What he really looked for was anything that would lead back to Arabia. In October 1924 one of Ibn Saud's captains

advanced to Mecca and attacked King Ali. Philby saw this as an
ideal situation which could bring him fame, if he could only mediate
the crisis.[53] He went to Jidda on his own, and upon arriving he was
reminded that legally he was still a serving British civil servant.
If he pursued his efforts to contact Ibn Saud against the wishes of
the British government, he could lose his pension. He wrote to Ibn
Saud requesting an interview. Ibn Saud's reply, though snubbing,
showed great wisdom:

> If there is something personal you are welcome
> to discuss it with me personally. If however
> there is something that pertains to the Hijaz
> and you wish to act as mediator, I would
> suggest your holding aloof from it. As you
> will observe, it is a purely Islamic problem
> in which your mediation will be uncalled for.[54]

King Ali asked him to stay but an attack of dysentary, compounded
by an injection through a dirty needle which caused an abcess,
resulted in Philby's evacuation to the hospital in Aden on January
3, 1925. Upon recovering he returned to England.

Philby and Ibn Saud (1925-1953)

The next trip Philby made to Jidda was not as a political
mediator, but as a businessman. He had been hired by Remy Fisher,
an entrepreneur who wanted to use Philby to establish concessions in
Arabia. Philby, no longer a civil servant, arrived in Jidda in
November 1925 and tried to contact Ibn Saud. The latter was in
the process of negotiating a treaty with the British and did not
reply until he had a first draft in hand. Ibn Saud arranged a
clandestine meeting with Philby on November 28, 1925. Philby reported
that he was representing a syndicate which wanted concessions for

a bank, a rail link between Mecca and Medina, and the development of
minerals. Ibn Saud's reply was affirmative, but all of that would
have to come in due time.[55] The wisdom of Ibn Saud was clear. He
was coming to power because of the religious fervor of his Wahhabi
faith and he was aware of the Ikhwan tribes' aversion to anyone or
anything not truly Moslem. Modernization would have to come in
carefully measured steps. Philby would be Ibn Saud's agent, but
not officially. The two separated. Ibn Saud was proclaimed King
of the Hijaz on January 8, 1926, and Philby set up his business
in Jidda.[56]

The next four years were not wholly satisfying for Philby.
He operated the 'Company of Explorers and Merchants in the Near and
Middle East.' His income was based on commissions earned selling
his wares and on royalties from his books. He wrote articles for
the Near East and India magazine in London, which continued to be
very critical of the British Mandate policies. His view was that Ibn
Saud had complete control over the Ikhwan and was capable of ruling
the entire peninsula. This type of discourse caused the Foreign
Office consternation, especially considering the fact that Philby
was at the same time drawing a government pension. Government
concern was lessened when it was perceived that even though Philby
was close to Ibn Saud, the latter was not taking him too seriously.[57]
Philby was able to achieve at least one form of gratification during
this period, that being his affairs with English women. Of course,
this caused his wife and mother anguish when, as part of his policy
of frankness, he told them. He wanted to maintain his family base
in England and Dora could be responsible for the mundane requirements

of a home. He wrote to her in 1928, "I am far too immersed in the persuit of my ambitions, my chief aim being to secure the immortality to be gained by the accomplishment of some great work...."[58] He was soon to take a step which would certainly facilitate his efforts.

St. John Philby became a member of the Muslim world on 7 July 1930. That date, according to the Muslim calendar, was the twelfth day of Rabilal Awwal, A.H. 1348; the birthday of the Prophet Muhammed. According to Philby, his decision to convert resulted from long contemplation on the philosophy of the Wahhabi creed and the unpleasant experience of a stroke during the hot summer of 1930.[59] Before taking that step alone, Philby invited David Van Der Meulen, the Minister from the Netherlands, to join him. "Let us become Muslims...you want to see more of the other side. We shall not lose anything and may gain by it."[60] Mr. Van Der Meulen declined. Ibn Saud made him an informal member of the Royal Court and bestowed on him the patromymic of Abdullah (Slave of God). In 1931 he made his first pilgrimage, and three years later he joined the royal family in the annual cleansing of the Ka'ba.[61] As a Moslem, Philby could travel anywhere in Arabia.

An ambition close to Philby's heart ever since he made his first exploration south of Riyadh in 1918, was to be the first westerner to explore the Rub al Khali. This vast, unchartered 'Empty Quarter' of southern Arabia was a real challenge, which, if he were to explore it, would certainly insure his fame. To Philby's chagrin, Bertram Thomas made a rapid crossing of the eastern part of the Rub al Khali from Salada to Doha in February 1931.[62] This trek was a surprise because Thomas had not received permission from Ibn Saud.

Philby was given permission to conduct his exploration in 1931 also, but was held back because of problems in the Asir-Yemen region (to be addressed below). He had to wait until December 1931 before he was again given permission.

The expedition began on January 7, 1932. The book which reports on the experience is The Empty Quarter (1933). The reader of this book will find that he is able to share nearly all of Philby's experiences and observations. There is a great amount of detail, with numerous Arabic names. Reading this work will provide knowledge which can only be surpassed by tracing Philby's trail. Through his scientific eyes the reader is exposed to the meteoric craters which were the basis for native lore of a city destroyed by God.[63] The physical composition and lay of the land is depicted without excessive scientific jargon. Annexes are provided for the scientific minded: there are the geological and palaeontological results which record his proof of previous water beds in the area; lists of the wide variety of animal specimens he brought back, and as he mapped his entire route, he included altitudes measured by his aneroid and hypsometer.[64]

As he had in his Heart of Arabia, he included a geneological chart of the tribe which inhabited the area. Halfway through his trip he had to contend with a near mutiny by his guides. They were afraid they would not be able to make the most dangerous crossing with the slow baggage train with all of Philby's equipment. Philby conceded to return to an oasis (Naifa) to send back the bulk of his baggage. Continuing with a small party with minimal supplies, Philby made his crossing of the 375 mile Abu Bahr gravel plain in

9 days, arriving at Sulaiyil on March 14th. It is at this point that he ends his story about the 'Empty Quarter'. The remainder of his trip to Mecca was along a pilgrim route through the highlands, and was much easier. He left Mecca in April and returned to England to write his book and claim his glory.[65] The Royal Geographical Society was elated to hear his speeches. Life was pleasant for the Philby family, with many parties and lectures to attend. At this time events elsewhere caused an American to seek out the now famous St. John Philby.

The California Standard Oil Company (SOCAL), which had obtained an oil concession in Bahrain at the end of 1928, struck oil in considerable quantities in May of 1931. St. John Philby was approached by Francis B. Loomis, former Under Secretary of State of the United States, to inquire about the possibilities of an oil concession for SOCAL in Arabia.[66] Philby's account of how oil was discovered and developed in Arabia, and his role in it, are presented in great detail in Arabian Oil Ventures (published after his death). The story shows Philby as a loyal informal agent of Ibn Saud, with his intent being to negotiate the best deal possible for Saudi Arabia.[67] The book is very readable and enlightening about his dealings with the various competitors between 1932-1938. The three essays which comprise the book report on the two unsuccessful competitor's attempts, as well as SOCAL negotiations. Philby believed that he was facilitating the introduction of the West to Saudi Arabia.

By 1932 Philby was doing well in business: he sold Fords to the royal family and other Saudis; and he negotiated with the Marconi Company in Italy to establish wireless (radio) stations.[68]

The introduction of the radio was initially resisted as a device of the devil. Ibn Saud demonstrated that it was acceptable by having portions of the Koran recited to the Ulema over the wireless--thus proving that it was an acceptable means of conveying the message of the Prophet.[69] The wisdom and leadership skills of Ibn Saud were continually tested.

After Ibn Saud gained control of the Hijaz, he realized that the continued concentration of the Ikhwan as a military force would inhibit his establishment of an effective government. He dispersed the Ikhwan throughout his territories in an effort to stabilize them in agricultural settlements and also to spread the faith. However, the introduction of infidels and their strange new devices, and a desire to spiritually cleanse the tribes in Iraq, Kuwait, and Transjordan led the Ikhwan to resume their raiding practices. Ibn Saud personally led the forces which fought the rebels at the battle of Sibila in March 1929. The Ikhwan were severely defeated. Their leader, Duwish was wounded but survived to try and rebuild the Ikhwan forces to fight again. He attempted to establish ties with Britain and Kuwait but was unsuccessful. Ibn Saud convinced the British and Kuwaiti leaders that they should not support the rebel Ikhwan. The borders were thereafter closed and by the end of December the majority of the remaining forces had deserted to the Saudi forces. The last of the rebel Ikhwan leaders surrendered to the British on January 10, 1930.[70] The Ikhwan were resettled and became the core of the National Guard.

When Ibn Saud established his control over the Hijaz, he also claimed the Asir region (the most fertile region in southwestern

Arabia) as a protectorate.[71] Hassan el-Idrisi, the ruler of the
Asir, was forced out of the region. He sought support from the
Imam Yehya, the ruler of Yemen. Border clashes escalated into major
combat over the oasis of Najran, the key to Yemen's coffee trade
with Arabia.[72] Ikhwan forces established their control over Najran
in the spring of 1932 and peace negotiations in the Yemeni Capital,
San'a, were commenced. By the spring of 1934 nothing had been
achieved through negotiation and on April 5th Ibn Saud had his sons,
Crown Prince Saud and Amir Faisal, lead their forces into Yemen.
Within three weeks Faisal had reached the port of Hudiada, the main
source of supply for San'a, forcing the Iman to sue for peace. Ibn
Saud displayed a great deal of wisdom and statesmanship in negotiating
the peace. He declared that all he wanted was a firm agreement on
boundaries in accordance with the status quo ante. The only cost
to the Imam was an indemnity to cover the Saudi campaign expenses.[73]
On June 23, 1932 the two parties signed the Treaty of Taif cementing
a new relationship between Saudi Arabia and Yemen.[74] During the
1935 pilgrimage, three Yemanis from the 7aidi tribe, armed with
daggers, tried to assassinate Ibn Saud and Crown Prince Saud but
only inflicted slight wounds before they were shot. Although the
assailants' passports had been signed by a son of the Imam, the
incident caused no damage to Saudi-Yemen relations. Security
measures for the King were, however, increased.[75]

By September 1934, Philby started to become distressed at
seeing what he thought to be a decline in Ibn Saud's effectiveness
as a ruler. The King had led the oil concession negotiations in
1933 and concluded the war with Yemen, but had since become pre-

occupied with hunting, travel among the tribes, and his concubines.
Philby observed huge debts accumulating from foreign creditors
(his own company particularly), while the King gave money away to
his favorites.[76] Despite these concerns, Philby refrained from
publicly criticizing Ibn Saud, and busied himself with travel and
exploration.

In February 1935, he explored the unmapped desert between Medina
and Buraida. In April, St. John and Dora Philby drove their car
from Mecca to England and returned in January 1936.[77] Ibn Saud
then commissioned Philby to map the southwestern portion of his
domain to aid in the delineation of boundaries with Yemen and the
Aden Protectorates. Philby's expedition started in April 1936 and
did not return until February 1937. The exploration was accomplished
by automobile and donkey, depending upon the trafficability of the
terrain. The record of the expedition was not published until 1952.
Arabian Highlands provides the reader a wealth of information, which
can best be appreciated by a student of the region. Philby
identified his proposed audience when he wrote that the book was
"for the expert and professional rather than the general reader."[78]
E.A. Speiser writing for Yale Review, concisely listed the subjects
covered: "Meteorological and geological observations; notes on
birds, insects, and plants; details of local agriculture and economy,
and, above all, studies of people, their customs and status,
religion and government, interrelationships and genealogies."[73]
Speiser commends the book because it is a study of a region just
prior to the onset of modernizing influences; and because it reflects
the calibre of its author. Philby classified the expedition as

"the greatest of all my Arabian journeys."[80] His expedition introduced the outside world to the demography of the region as well as the topography, but his archaeological finds were the most significant scientific aspect of his journey. There was, however, a political aspect to the trip which caused Ibn Saud some immediate embarrassment, and future political battles. Philby had extended his exploration beyond Arabian territory and travelled on through Yemen to Mukalla on the southern coast of the Aden Protectorates. He was escorted throughout his journey by an armed guard provided by Ibn Saud. Philby was not a favored individual in the eyes of the British officers in Aden, and his open disregard of their authority by extending Saudi arms into their territory caused a furor in diplomatic channels.[81] As a result of Philby's expedition, however, the British and Yemeni governments obtained data which revealed that there were large, populated, areas not under anyone's control. The British in Aden and the Yemeni government, sent out forces to extend their boundaries. Before 1937 Aden claimed 42,000 square miles; after 1937, it claimed 112,000 square miles.[82] Philby publicly opposed British claims and military actions in the area.

There was one subject on which Britain's and Philby's positions nearly coincided: the Palestine problem. This was an issue which caused Philby to question the worth of his relationship with Saudi Arabia. Between May 1937 and May 1940 he supported various British proposals for a solution to the question and set forth many of his own. As was stated in the Introduction, the evolution of his plans and the reactions of Ibn Saud and the Jewish, British, and American

governments are too complex and significant to present within
this chapter. Therefore chapters two and three will address Philby's
and Ibn Saud's involvement in the Palestine question. In 1939 and
1940 Philby assumed a political stance which caused him to be
absented from Saudi Arabia until 1945.

When the Nazis moved on Prague, Philby advocated negotiations
with Germany.[83] He opposed the war and spoke openly about the
probability of Britain losing it. His proclamations were of serious
concern to both the Saudi and British governments. When Philby told
Ibn Saud that he was going to America, Ibn Saud informed the British
government. Philby was to travel via Bombay to America. He set
sail on August 3, 1940. Upon his arrival in Karachi, the British
arrested Philby and shipped him to England. He was imprisoned
under the Defense of the Realm Act, Sec. 18B. By March of 1941
he was released and considered a 'harmless fanatic'.[84] During
the rest of the war years he tried politics, and writing, but had
no luck. By mid 1945, his only hope for financial gain was to
return to Arabia.

When Philby returned to Jidda in July 1945, he was summoned to
Ibn Saud's court to resume his normal place. His services were still
of value to the King, who gave him a 'jariya', a 16- year old
beauty. Philby (60 years old) called her Rozy. In 1946, Mitchell
Cotts bought the company Philby had run, and he was retained at a
much higher salary. Rozy gave birth to two sons; one in 1947 and
the other in 1948, but both died before they were a year old. In
October 1950, Philby decided to explore the eastern part of the
Rub al Khali. He was denied permission because there were disputes

with the British over oil rights, and the King did not want the
problems he had had in Aden in 1936.[85] Philby then received permission
to explore the Midian region in the northwest. With this expedition,
he completed his coverage of every major region in Arabia. He was
accompanied by a renowned epigraphist, Monseigneur Gonzaque Ryckmans.
By February of 1952 they had covered 3,000 miles and had collected
13,000 new inscriptions.[86] During the next year he led a mining
survey team in Midian which determined that there was a possibility
of gold in the region. He also completed his mapping of the entire
area. His book, The Land of Midian (1957) contained the same sort
of detail as Arabian Highlands. Philby also wrote an earlier article
of the same title for the Middle East Journal (Spring 1955). In just
fourteen pages Philby presented a clear description of his explorations
and major finds in the region. He contributed a great deal of
scientific information to be added to the history of Arabia; but,
for those of us interested in people and governments, his Arabian
Jubilee was his greatest contribution.

St. John Philby was commissioned to write the history of Ibn
Saud's rule for the occasion of the King's 50th (lunar) anniversary
in July of 1950. Arabian Jubilee is his testimonial to Abdul-Aziz-
ibn-Saud. St. John Philby considered his relationship with Ibn
Saud to be parallel to that of his namesake, who also heralded the
coming of a King.[87] He does not simply provide a chronicle, but a
combination biography and personal narrative. His sources were
official British records, the memories of Saudi family members, and
Arabic manuscripts which are credited in his preface. He escorts
the reader through time to trace Ibn Saud's rise to absolute rule

and assesses the impact of modernization and time on a great man.
The religious and physical forces of the Ikhwan tribes provided the
foundation for Ibn Saud's rule. Philby addresses Ibn Saud's battles
with Ibn Rashid and King Hussein in the first six chapters, and
provides a clear appreciation of the complex interactions of Arab
families with the Turkish and British governments. The next few
chapters deal with Ibn Saud's program for political stabilization and
the introduction of western means for modernization. He devised
and implemented a program which settled mixed communities drawn
from different tribes and held together by a sense of religious brother
hood. By 1930, tribal raids had become a thing of the past.[88] Ibn
Saud personally administered the introduction of modernizing
influences such as schools, hospitals, better roads, the automobile,
and oil exploration. Philby's only real criticism was that the patri-
archal monarch had "never seemed to realize the necessity of equipping
them (his people) with the administrative machinery required for
their guidance amid the pitfalls of the future."[89] When it came to
politics and handling his people, Ibn Saud had no peers.

Chapter XIV, The Miracle, concerns the discovery and impact
of oil. Philby describes the key personalities (including his own)
participating in this most significant part of Arabian history. He
again states his assessment of the excessive concentration of power
and responsibility in the Ministry of Finance; and includes a
solution: "The institution of collective ministerial responsiblity
would thus seem to be the only way of restoring equilibrium..."
This, in fact was implemented in 1954 and strengthened in 1958.[90]

Chapter XVII deals with The Palestine Problem.   According

to Philby, "the true basis of Arab hostility...is xenophobia, an
instinctive perception of the fact that the vast majority of the
central and eastern European Jews,....are not Semites at all."[91]
The positions taken by the Arabs are assessed, as is Philby's plan
(to be discussed in greater detail below). He concludes this chapter
by expressing his opinion that "the Jews have not a shadow of legal
or historical right to go to Palestine;" and that the matter should
be referred to the International Court of Justice for a ruling.

The final chapter, Sunset,' is a capstone review of the manner
in which Ibn Saud ruled. Philby addressed the role of Abdullah
Sulaimann, the Minister of Finance, in balance with the King's
centralization of all control. The two worked closely together from
the beginning when the wealth of the royal house was counted in
sheep and rice. Ibn Saud ruled Arabia; while Sulaimann, more and
more, assumed control of administration and finances. As the book
ends, Ibn Saud is nearly seventy years old, is tired and worn down
by the burden of rule, and fears the North Koreans as the yellow
men of Gog and Magog who portend the approach of doomsday. Ibn Saud
died on November 9, 1953 and Philby lost his patron.

Philby After Ibn Saud (1953-1960)

The last 'history' book Philby wrote was Saudi Arabia, published
in 1955. It was a "chronicle of the acts and achievements of a
great dynasty, which has ruled in Arabia for five centuries..."
This history is extremely informative but may cause some
consternation to those who want to trace his sources. In his
introduction he identifies his major sources as Arab historians
and even recommends some works by others; but there are no footnotes

and there is no bibliography. St. John Philby expected his readers
to accept his work as truth...as seen by him. None of his European
reviewers had any problems in doing just that.

After Ibn Saud's death, Philby fell from grace in the royal
court. In his foreward to Saudi Arabia, he had pronounced a judgment
on Ibn Saud's reign and the prospects for his successors. In April
1955 he was told that his continual criticisms of the royal family
were not going to be tolerated, and he was told to leave. He moved
to Beriut with Rozy and their two surviving sons. Dora knew of
Rozy, but not of the four sons. There he stayed until May of 1956
when a reconiciliation with the Saudi government was arranged on the
condition that he stop his open criticism.[92] He maintained his home
in Beirut while alternating trips to Riyadh, England, and Lebanon.
Dora died in England on June 25th 1957; she had last seen her husband
in 1954. Philby was a visiting professor at the American University in
Beirut and students recall that "he was lively, approachable, conversa-
tional." His last few years were spent writing his autobiography, Forty
Years in the Wilderness and drafting his Arabian Oil Ventures. Derek
Hopwood aptly concluded, "His tragedy was that of every man who lives to
see his own familiar world crumble away and his return to a changed Arabia
was a sadder fate than his exile."[93] St. John Philby, at the age of
75, and after a full night of being the life of many parties,
succumbed to heart trouble and died on September 30, 1960. His last
words were, "I am bored."[94]

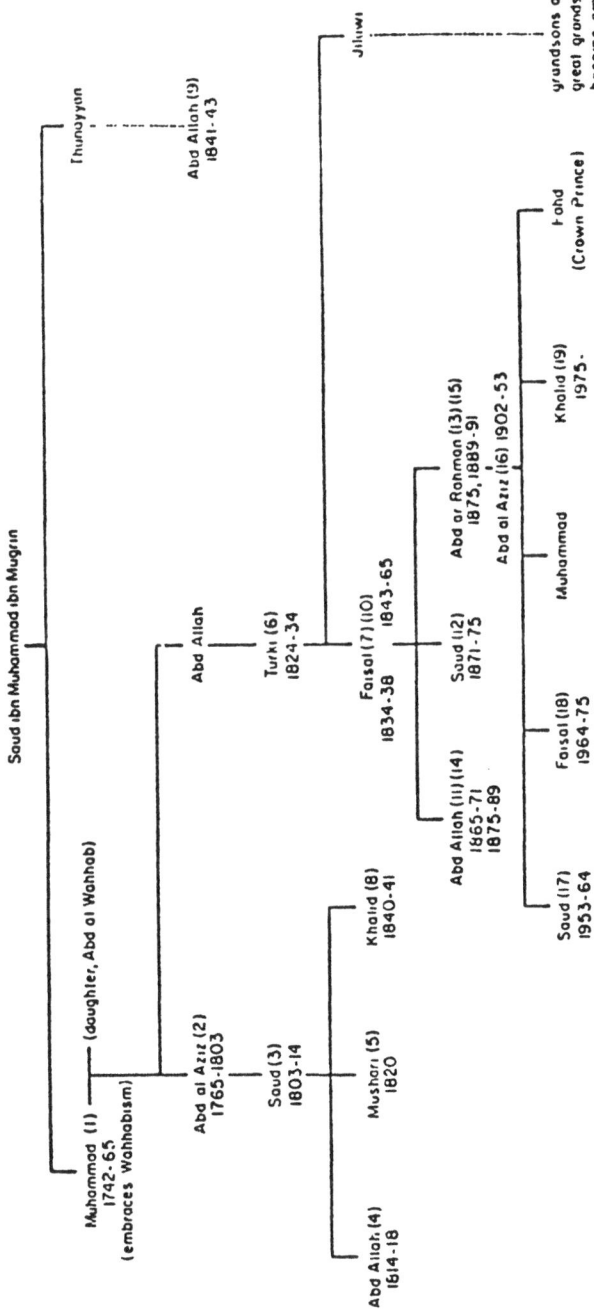

Figure 2: House of Saud

Note--Numerous brothers of rulers have been omitted, including thirty four brothers of King Khalid Numbers indicate order of rule, and dates indicate period of rule

Source: Richard F. Nyrop. _Area Handbook for Saudia Arabia._ Washington, D.C.: American University Foreign Area Studies, 1977.

Chapter One Notes

1. Elizabeth Monroe. Philby of Arabia. (London; Faber and Faber, 1973), p. 19.

2. Ibid., p. 26; H. St. John Philby. Arabian Days: An Autobiography. (London; Robert Hale Limited, 1948), pp. 31-32.

3. Ibid., p. 31.

4. Ibid., p. 34.

5. Ibid., p. 44.

6. Ibid., p. 49.

7. Ibid.

8. H. St. John Philby. Arabian Jubilee. (New York: The John Day Co., 1953), p. 52.

9. Monroe, p. 60.

10. Richard F. Nyrop, Area Handbook for Saudi Arabia, Washington, D.C.: U.S. Government Printing Office, 1977, p. 121.

11. Ibid., p. 120.

12. Ameen Rihani, Maker of Modern Arabia, (Boston: Houghton Mifflin Co., 1928), p. 237.

13. Nyrop, p. 121.

14. Ibid., p. 25.

15. J. G. Lorimer, Gazetter of the Persian Gulf, Oman, and Central Arabia, (Shannon, Ireland; Irish University Press, 1970), Vol. 16, p. 1054.

16. Ibid., p. 1072.

17. Ibid., p. 1089.

18. Ibid., p. 1097.

19. Ibid., pp. 1109-1120.

20. Philby, Jubilee, p. 6.

21. Ibid., p. 11.

22. Nyrop, p. 30.

23. Philby, Arabian Jubilee, p. 43.

24. Sharif Hussein turned on the Ottomans and agreed with the British to lead an Arab revolt in return for Arab independence after the war. See Elie Kedourie. In the Anglo-Arab Labyrinth: The McMahon-Husayn Correspondence and its Interpretations 1914-1939. (London: Cambridge University Press, 1976).

25. Ibid., p. 53.

26. Monroe, p. 67.

27. Ibid., p. 70. For a more thorough discussion of why the British supported Hussein see Gary Troeller, The Birth of Saudi Arabia: Britain and the Rise of the House of Sa'ud, (London: CASS, 1976), pp. 75-83.

28. Ibid., p. 74.

29. Ibid., p. 80.

30. Ibid., pp. 84-87.

31. H. St. John Philby. The Heart of Arabia. Vol. II, (London: Constable, 1922) p. 307.

32. Philby, Arabian Jubilee, pp. 32-41.

33. Philby, Arabia of the Wahhabi, (London: Constable, 1928), Preface.

34. Ibid., p. 335.

35. Monroe, p. 102.

36. Ibid., p. 104.

37. Lorimer, Part 1B, p. 981.

38. Monroe, p. 106.

39. Ibid., p. 111.

40. Ibid., p. 116.

41. Ibid., p. 123.

42. Rihani, pp. 165-169.

43. H. C. Armstrong, Lord of Arabia. (London: Arthur Baker Ltd., 1934), p. 194.

44. Troeller, pp. 174-175.

45. Amin Rihani was Cox's translator. His diary records the observation: "We take from Ibn Sa'ud to satisfy Iraq, and we take from Trans-Jordan to placate Ibn Sa'ud." Rihani, p. 96.

46. Troeller, p. 181.

47. The British Company did not find oil and let the concession expire in 1928, owing Ibn Saud £6,000 in back rent. See Philby, Arabian Jubilee, pp. 68-69.

48. Monroe, p. 125.

49. Ibid., p. 128. Philby wrote a chapter in Sir Alexander Kennedy's book PETRA: Its History and Monuments. (London: Country Life, 1925).

50. Ibid., pp. 129-136.

51. Ibid., p. 135.

52. Philby, Arabian Jubilee, p. 76. Also, Sir Reader Bullard, The Camels Must Go: An Autobiography. (London: Faber and Faber, 1961), pp. 138-139.

53. Monroe, p. 141.

54. Ibid., p. 143.

55. Ibid., p. 147.

56. Ibid.; Philby, Arabian Jubilee, pp. 72-78.

57. Ibid., p. 150 and P.R.O.F.O./371/13010, E484/484/91. Jedda report for December 1928.

58. Ibid., p. 152.

59. Philby, Arabian Days, pp. 278-280.

60. David Van Der Meulen. The Wells of Ibn Saud. (New York: Praeger, 1957), p. 28.

61. Monroe, p. 167.

62. Ibid., p. 176.

63. Philby, The Empty Quarter. (London: Holt, 1933), p. 365.

64. Ibid., p. 407.

65. Monroe, p. 187.

66. Philby, Arabian Oil Ventures. (Washington: Middle East Institute, 1964), p. 77.

67. Ibid., Forward.

68. Monroe, p. 207.

69. Philby, Arabian Jubilee, p. 91.

70. Christine Helms, The Cohesion of Saudi Arabia (Baltimore: John Hopkins University Press, 1981), pp. 250-271.

71. Philby, Arabian Jubilee, p. 184.

72. Monroe, p. 175.

73. Philby, Arabian Jubilee, p. 186.

74. George Lenczowski, The Middle East in World Affairs. (Ithaca: Cornell University Press, 1980), p. 579.

75. Philby, Arabian Jubilee, p. 188-189.

76. Monroe, p. 212.

77. Ibid., p. 213.

78. Philby. Arabian Highlands. (Ithica: Cornell, 1952), p. X.

79. E. A. Speiser. Yale Review. December 1951, p. 620.

80. Philby. Highlands, p. 708.

81. Monroe, p. 217.

82. Ibid., p. 303.

83. Ibid., p. 219.

84. Ibid., p. 230.

85. Ibid., p. 251.

86. Ibid., p. 265.

87. Philby. Arabian Jubilee, p. 3.

88. Ibid., p. 95.

89. Ibid., p. 97.

90. Philby. "The New Statute of the Council of Ministers."
Middle East Journal. Vol. XII 1958, No. 3., p. 318.

91. Monroe, p. 204.

92. Ibid., p. 286.

93. Derek Hopwood. The Arabian Peninsula. ed. (London:
George Allen and Unwin Ltd., 1972), p. 17.

94. Monroe, p. 295.

CHAPTER TWO

PHILBY, IBN SAUD AND PALESTINE, 1936-1939:

THE PROBLEM AND PHILBY'S SOLUTION

In 1925, St. John Philby divorced himself from the British

Civil Service and assumed the role of liaison officer between Ibn

Saud and the western world. His developing relationship with Ibn

Saud was variously judged as indicated in the British legation's

report in 1933:

> He was for some time in and after 1924 a thorn
> in the side of British authorities and was
> described in 1925 as clinging tenaciously to
> his religion, "a simple dualism in which the
> spirit of darkness is represented by His
> Majesty's Government." Need now no longer be
> regarded as anti-British, except that he would
> still sympathise with Ibn Saud in any quarrel
> with His Majesty's Government, and will still
> rail on occasion against the British Empire
> as a system. He would as soon sell British
> goods as Standard Oil or Ford cars and he got
> Ibn Saud's wireless contract for Marconi's
> in 1931. His influence with the King has been
> exaggerated by some into a legend, while many
> still believe him to be a British political
> agent. He has much access to the King and the
> King values his advice on certain occasions,
> but he presents no appearance of being in Ibn
> Saud's confidence on major political occasions.[1]

The King looked to Philby for advice on western means to materially

improve the lives of his people. For Ibn Saud politics were mainly an

Arab affair and Philby's advice was not needed. In 1930, Philby

became a Muslim and an informal member of King Ibn Saud's Divan (privy

council). He participated fully in the King's council meetings. Ibn

Saud equated his council to the British Parliament and once said "we

discuss everything here in complete democratic freedom, and we even

have our official opposition. Philby is that!"[2] The Palestine prob-

lem prored the British legation report and Ibn Saud's observation to
be correct. This chapter will address St. John Philby's efforts in
the search for a solution to the seemingly inrreconcilable conflict
between the Zionists and the Arabs. In order to appreciate Philby's
efforts, they must be considered within the context of the complex
Zionist, Arab, British and American relations between 1936 and 1939.

The Problem, as seen by Arabs and Zionists

Jewish immigration and land acquisition in Palestine started
increasing rapidly after Hitler assumed power in March 1933. Jewish
immigration into Palestine between 1933-1936 totaled (net) 163,098.[3]
In March 1936, Arab Nationalists in Egypt and Syria, after large
demonstrations and strikes, were promised independence; the economy
in Palestine was in a recession; Fascist radio broadcasts from Italy
were full of anti-British propoganda aimed at the Arabs, and the
Palestinian Arab nationalists began their own movement.

The Palestinian Arabs decided that the Jewish immigration and
land acquisition in Palestine must stop. On April 24, 1936 the Arab
Higher Committee was formed and Haj Amin el Husseni, the Mufti of
Jerusalem, became its president. The Higher Committee announced
that its objective was the prohibition of further Jewish immigration,
forbiddance of land transfer from Arabs to Jews, and the replacement
of the Mandate by a national government.[4] It ordered a general Arab
strike in hopes of coercing the British into meeting the demands.
Partial success was achieved when the British approved only 4,500
of the 11,200 Jewish visa requests. The Colonial Secretary J. H.
Thomas informed Parliament that a Royal Commission would investigate

the cause of unrest, but only after order was restored. The
Commission's terms of reference for their investigation were such
that the Mandate and its policies were not to be challenged. This
inflamed the Arabs and the strike evolved into open guerrilla warfare.
The Jewish community's economy was damaged somewhat, however, the
Arabs were doing more harm to themselves. When the Palestinian
Arabs stopped work the Jewish immigrants were able to replace them.
Jewish farms increased production to make up for the reduced Arab
production. The Arab port of Jaffa lost a great deal of its normal
traffic to the Jewish operated facility at Tel-Aviv. The tourist
trade was reduced and unemployment was raised. Britain sent more
troops. By November the Arab Higher Committee began to feel the
economic and British troop pressures. In October the Arab rulers
of Iraq, Transjordan, Saudi Arabia and Yemen issued notes calling
for an end to the violence and to have faith in "the good intentions
of our friend Great Britain, who had declared that she will do
justice."[5] Thus the Palestinian Arabs were able to stop fighting
and save face and the Royal Commission was able to begin its
investigation in November. The Commission was, with some hesitation
on the part of the Arabs, able to conclude its investigation by the
end of January, 1937.

While the Royal Commission was compiling its report, the Jewish
Agency was trying to establish contacts with Arab leaders or their
advisors in order to convey its views on the Palestinian situation
to them. David Ben-Gurion, Chairman of the Zionist and Jewish
Agency Executive, met first with Fuad Bey Hamzah in the latter's
home in Beirut on April 13, 1937.[6] Hamzah was a Druze of Lebanese

birth, who spoke fluent English, and had graduated from the American
College of Beirut and the Jerusalem Law School. He was Ibn Saud's
Director of Foreign Affairs. Ben-Gurion asked Hamzah how Saudi Arabia
viewed the Palestinian problem. Stating that he was unauthorized
to speak for anyone but himself, Hamzah wanted to discuss the issue
in terms of Palestinian Arab claims and Jewish responses.[7] Hamzah
stated that the Palestinian Arabs considered the three key issues to
be immigration, land and political rule. The economic prosperity
gained by the influx of Jews would mean nothing if the Arabs became
a minority and lost control of their country. It was impractical
to believe the Jewish argument that it was possible to establish
a government based on the non-domination of one group over another
regardless of the population ratio. As long as the Jews constituted
a minority in Palestine, they might support such a position. When
they became a majority, Jews would certainly seek to dominate the
Arabs. Ben-Gurion thought that too narrow a view. Any agreement
reached by the Arabs and Jews would certainly be guaranteed by the
much larger Arab states on Palestine's borders. In the larger
context, the land in Palestine constituted less than two percent
of all Arab lands, and the Arab population was only three percent
of the world's Arabs. For the Jews on the other hand, "it was a
question of their national past and future.....there was no comparing
the value of Erez Israel for the Arabs with the importance it held
for the Jewish people."[8]

Hamzah asked if Ben Gurion was trying to argue that Palestine
should be opened to the seventeen million Jews of the world, thereby
creating a desire for more territory. The reply was an historical

dissertation on the Zionist movement. Not all Jews wanted to leave their present homes, but for those who did, Israel was their only choice. It had been agreed that immigration would be limited by the economic absorptive capacity and the promise not to dispossess the Arabs. Jewish technology and industry were increasing the absorption and it was impossible to state a number for the ultimate limit. When pressed for a number by Hamzah, Ben-Gurion estimated that the coastal region could provide settlement for 100,000 families. When Hamzah expressed his belief that the Royal Commission would provide answers to the problem, Ben-Gurion voiced his doubts. He believed that the problem would remain unresolved until the Jews and Arabs came to an agreement. The Jews regretted that no Arab statesman had been found who could see the solution in terms of a mutually beneficial partnership.

Ben-Gurion asked whether Ibn Saud, who was a great statesman in his country, was also capable of penetrating to the heart of issues remote from his land and of expressing an opinion about how to solve the Jewish-Arab question in Erez Israel.[9] He did not want Ibn Saud to be the judge in this issue, but he valued the opinion of such a great Arab figure and thought it beneficial for Ibn Saud to hear the Jewish position. Hamzah stated that Ibn Saud was capable of understanding the problem, but he would have to confer with the King before stating whether such a meeting could occur. Hamzah recommended that in the meantime the Jewish Agency representative should meet with Crown Prince Saud and Sheikh Yusuf Yasin (the King's private secretary) who were travelling to London for the coronation of King George VI. Hamzah promised that he would make such a recommendation to the Prince. Also, he would report Ben-Gurion's remarks to Ibn Saud. Ben-Gurion went to London and arranged to meet with two Englishmen who were familiar with Ibn Saud: St. John Philby and Captain H. C. Armstrong.

It must be noted here that Philby had just returned to London from his mapping expedition in the southwestern region of Saudi Arabia. He had extended his travels into the Aden protectorate, and as he was escorted by some of Ibn Saud's armed men, he greatly perturbed the British officials who directed him to leave immed.ately. Philby chose to explore more of the protectorate and Yemen which further aggravated the British and the Imam of Yemen. Philby had caused Ibn Saud a good deal of diplomatic trouble with his southern neighbors, but he believed that the knowledge gained about the region was worth it.[10]

Ben-Gurion met Philby for lunch at the Athenaeum Club on May 18, 1937. As the two discussed the Palestine problem, Philby asserted that after the Royal Commission published its report the "war" would resume. The only reason there was a peace at the moment was because of Ibn Saud's intervention with the Mufti of Jerusalem. According to Philby: Ibn Saud was opposed to the Zionist policies and had stated that Jewish immigration was "talm" (an injustice).[11] Nevertheless, he wanted to give the Royal Commission a chance. Philby was of the opinion that England wanted to make Palestine a Crown Colony. His contention was that the English government was using the Jews to its advantage and that England should get out of the country which rightly belonged to the Arabs. Ben-Gurion argued that the Jews had a right to return to Palestine; they would fight for that right if necessary, but would rather have a treaty agreement

with the Arabs. Such a treaty would have three elements:

1. Jewish immigration unrestricted in numbers or for
    political reasons, with the exception of the non-
    eviction of Arabs;

2. The country's independence in internal affairs;

3. Ties with an Arab federation or confederation. [12]

Ben-Gurion believed that if the Jews and Arabs reached an agreement

the British would then support it. Philby was very pessimistic

about British willingness to relinquish control of Palestine. However

he believed that if an agreement were based on complete realism

with no possibility of English intervention, Ibn Saud would consent

to it. He added that Ibn Saud was the only Arab leader who could head

the Arab confederation to which Ben-Gurion had referred. In Philby's

opinion, Palestine and Transjordan should be one state and under

Ibn Saud's rule. Emir Abdullah of Transjordan was not a bad man,

but he was not a real ruler. He was a British puppet. Philby

based his opinion of Abdullah on his service with him between 1921

and 1924.

Ben-Gurion confessed that he had not considered Ibn Saud in

such a role. In fact he did not believe any of the Jews or Arabs

of the region would accept the rule of the Bedouin King. [13] According

to Ben-Gurion, Philby's response was, "Leave the Arabs to me, we'll

manage with them." To say the least, Philby was very prideful. When

asked if Ibn Saud would agree to Jewish immigration, Philby said

that he would. If there were an Arab federation it would need develop-

ment and for that Ibn Saud would see the Jews as an asset. Arabia

made its meager living from pilgrims. Subsidies from England meant subservience. Money was needed and the Jews could supply it.

As Philby presented the situation to Ben-Gurion, England was the real danger. Ibn Saud was concerned that England would turn his country into a British colony. There was British pressure to the north out of the Aden Protectorate. Ibn Saud would resist, of course, but Philby expressed the view that England would not be content with Aden. Philby then concluded his talk with Ben-Gurion suggesting that a meeting with "some of Ibn Saud's people" might be good. He would let Ben-Gurion know.[14]

As was mentioned earlier, Ben-Gurion had arranged to meet with two Englishmen. The second was Captain Harold Courtney Armstrong. He was an Orientalist who had written biographies on Mustafa Kemal and Ibn Saud. His book on the latter, Lord of Arabia (1934), was a collection of colorful tales which glorified Ibn Saud's exploits and portrayed him as an Islamic puritan with a divine mission.[15]

When Ben-Gurion left Philby, he went to the Royal Automobile Club for his second engagement. Captain H. C. Armstrong was described by Ben-Gurion as an Arabic speaking friend of Ibn Saud who "spoke like a British imperialist: he was not concerned either about the Arabs or the Jews, and he said so frankly."[16] Ben-Gurion told Armstrong that inter-Arab quarreling was preventing any Arab from entering into treaty negotiations with the Jews for fear of being denounced as a traitor. The situation demanded an Arab with influence who would be willing to "delve deeply into the matter",[17] i.e., listen to the Jewish position. He asked Armstrong if he believed that Ibn Saud was such a man. Armstrong replied that:

> "Ibn Saud was a wise, cautious and honest man.
> He adopted a realistic approach to things,
> took the facts into account. Though he was
> a devout Moslem, he was not a fanatic. He
> smoked in private. He was a truly frank
> person. He never deceived anyone. If he
> was asked something he might refuse to answer,
> but if he said yes or no, his yes was a yes
> and his no was a no."

According to Armstrong, Ibn Saud decided everything on his own, and no one could act in his name.

Armstrong portrayed Philby in a very negative light. Although a friend of Ibn Saud's, Philby certainly was not his political advisor. Armstrong's observation of Philby's relationship with the King's entourage is particularly interesting.

> "Philby was hated....because he was rude to
> them. He was given to cursing and abusing
> people. The Wahhabis were careful not to
> use profanity, and Ibn Saud himself would
> never curse anyone. He might slap a man in
> the face, or cut off his hands, but he would
> not curse him, and that is why Philby was
> disliked, since he was a Wahhabi Moslem."[18]

As for arranging a meeting with Ibn Saud, Armstrong did not believe it would be possible until after the Royal Commission published its report. However, he would contact Ibn Saud's representatives to determine whether a meeting would be worthwhile. Two weeks later Ben-Gurion received a letter from Armstrong stating that after repeated attempts he was unable to arrange a meeting, and that further attempts might be counter productive.[19]

On May 26th, before receiving Armstrong's negative reply, Ben-Gurion had a second meeting with St. John Philby at the Athenaeum. Philby told Ben-Gurion that he had tried to convince Yusuf Yasin that the three of them should meet. Yasin's reply was that Ibn Saud had directed him not to speak to anyone on political matters,

and therefore such a meeting was impossible. Philby was not willing
to let such an opportunity pass. He proposed to Ben-Gurion that the
two of them should pursue the subject, and, if an agreement were
reached, it should be conveyed in writing to Ibn Saud, with a
summary published in the newspapers. Ben-Gurion rejected the idea
of publishing a letter. He was pursuing the subject as a private
individual. If he were to publish anything it would be seen as a
Jewish Agency commitment. Philby argued that because of his
reputation as a supporter of the Arabs, any declaration he might
make in favor of the Jews would make a great impression. Ben-Gurion
agreed to look at Philby's draft of an agreement, stipulating that
although they agreed on some points there were still some deep-seated
differences. Philby produced his draft that afternoon.

The eleven points of the draft agreement (Appendix A) boil down
to four key elements:

1. A denouncement of the British and their preferential
   position in Palestine;

2. The opening of Immigration to everyone, subject only
   to absorptive capacity as determined by a commission
   composed of Arabs and Jews acting under a League of
   Nations sanction;

3. The establishment of a Greater Palestine by joining
   Palestine with Transjordan and having a plebiscite
   to determine whether Abdullah, Ibn Saud or an
   elected President would head a monarchy or a
   republican government;

4. The guarantee of Jewish freedom in religious and
   cultural matters.[20]

Ben-Gurion wrote a response to Philby on May 31 (Appendix B).
The only points on which they were in agreement were those which
rejected the idea of partition, called for freedom of Jewish religious

and cultural expression, prohibited preferential treatment for
external powers, and called for a combined Palestine and Transjordan.
He believed that immigration had to be controlled by Jews and opened
only to the Jews since it was their efforts which increased the
absorptive capacity of the land. The Jews did not want to finance
the immigration of other races.[21] As for the form of government,
the Jews wanted a guarantee of non-domination, i.e., complete parity
in government between Jews and Arabs, irrespective of population ratios
Ben-Gurion hoped that a parity agreement would not be necessary for
ever.

> "the time will come when Arabs and Jews will work
> together in mutual confidence, and the lines of
> division will become other than racial ones.
> This consciousness of a common citizenship will
> develop gradually as a result of economic coopera-
> tion, but until it has developed, and until the
> present racial suspicionsness has disappeared,
> it is necessary to have some arrangement which
> will prevent either race from being dominated
> by the other."[22]

According to Ben-Gurion, if the Mandate were to be abolished
there would still be a need for a League of Nations guarantee in
addition to that provided by the Arabs, although Ben-Gurion did not
have much faith in the League of Nations. Ben-Gurion also took
issue with Philby's attempt to exclude the British totally. He
believed that Britain's vital interests would have to be considered
in any Jewish-Arab agreement or England would not approve it.[23]
Philby did not reply to Ben-Gurion.

Obviously Ben-Gurion and Philby viewed the situation from very
different perspectives. Each had his own concept for a solution.
Philby envisioned Ibn Saud as the guarantor, if not the ruler, of

a Greater Palestine which would allow the Jewish people to settle and help develop the economy. The Jews would have their representatives in government to protect their interests and recourse to the League of Nations or the International Court of Justice if they were not fairly governed. Ben-Gurion on the other hand, envisioned a free flow of Jews into Palestine, restricted only by an absorptive capacity defined by the Jewish Agency. Parity in government, economic cooperation and the spectre of Britain or the League of Nations were required to guarantee the peace until the two peoples learned to live together. The central point concerned who was going to govern, Arab or Jew. A mutual understanding was not attained at the Athenaeum Club in England, nor was there one in Palestine.

The Peel Commission

The Royal Commission, headed by William Robert Wellesley, Lord Peel, former Secretary of State for India, conducted their investigation in Palestine from early November, 1936, until the third week in January, 1937. The Commission had been instructed to determine what the "legitimate" Arab and Jewish grievances were and "to make recommendations for their removal and for the prevention of their recurrence."[24] The Royal Commission (Peel) Report on Palestine was released on July 7, 1937.[25] The report stated that Arab grievances about Jewish immigration and land acquisition were, under the terms of the Mandate, unjustified. However, meeting the obligations given to the Jews could only be accomplished by British repression of the Arabs. The Comission found that the Palestine Mandate had been premised on the assumption that the Arabs would acquiesce in the establishment of the Jewish National Home because of the material advantages. Obviously the Arabs proved the assumption to be invalid. The Arabs were increasingly demanding their independence, and the Jews were adamant about the development of their National Home. The intensity of the relationship between the Arabs and Jews increased exponentially as the pressure mounted for the latten's co-religionists in Nazi territories. In the opinion of the Royal Commission there was no hope of establishing a representative government, and therefore the Palestine Mandate was unworkable.[26]

The Commission assessed the three major proposals for a settlement that were put before it. The Arab Higher Committee recommended the establishment of an independent Arab State. This was dismissed because of the fear that the rights of the Jews might not be safeguarded. It was recalled that the Mufti had asserted that the 400,000 Jews in Palestine could not be assimilated and that their fate would have to be left "to the future".[27] That was the Palestinian Arab extremist view. The Jewish extremist or "Revisionist" proposal was the establishment of a Jewish government over Palestine and Transjordan. That too was rejected as not being feasible because the Arab world would not stand for it. The Jewish Agency proposal was for a parity scheme of government, whereby the seats of power would be split on a 50/50 basis...." the Jews would never claim more than that equal number, whatever the future ratio between Arab and Jewish population might become."[28] The Commission evaluated that proposal as not being feasible either because the Arabs and Jews would invariably find themselves in a deadlock on major issues. Also, the Arabs would never give up the advantage they enjoyed in being the majority for a _promise_ that the Jews would never assume control when they became the majority. Having rejected all of the proposals put before it, the Commission came up with its own.

Partition was the recommended answer. As soon as possible there should be established separate and sovereign Jewish and Arab States, and a British mandatory zone. (See map at Appendix C). The Jewish State would take about 20% of Palestine and would include Galilee, the Jezreel Valley, and the Coastal plain to a point midway between Gaza and Jaffa. The British mandate zone would encompass the Holy Places of Jerusalem and Bethlehem, and a corridor to the Mediterranean at Jaffa. The British would also maintain a mandate over the north-west corner of the Gulf of Aqabah. Temporary British control would be maintained in the towns of Safad, Tiberias, Acre, and Haifa. The Arabs would have the rest of Palestine, the port city of Jaffa, and would be united with Transjordan. Both Arabs and Jews were to have free access to the ports of Haifa and Aqabah. Britain was to have preferential treaties with both states. The Jews were to give subventions to the Arabs. Britain was to grant the Arabs £2,000,000 (£1=$5 in 1937). Jewish land purchases in the Arab state were to be prohibited during the transition period. Jewish immigration was to be restricted to the absorptive capacity of the area designated for the Jewish state.

The Royal Commission concluded that "Half a loaf is better than no bread" (Appendix D). The major advantages to the drastic provisions were that neither group would dominate the other, the Arabs would achieve independence and the Jewish National Home would be an independent state. The British were to enjoy benefits also, although they were not discussed in the report. England would be released from its commitment for troops to keep the peace, while it maintained its economic and strategic ties with the states.[29]

The Royal Commission realized that there would be opposition to the plan and identified certain "palliatives" which were to ease the pain if partition was rejected. Jewish settlement was to be restricted to the coastal plains. Also, immigration was to be restricted for five years with a "political high level" of 12,000 a year. If violence erupted, marital law was to be enforced, the police system reorganized, and rigid press controls imposed.

The British government issued a Statement of Policy which generally agreed with the Royal Commission's conclusion.[30] Parliament had a heated debate which resulted in deferring the partition plan to the League of Nations as the overall responsible body. The League of Nations Mandate Commission favored futher study and planned to dispatch an investigative commission of its own. It also reminded Britain that the Mandate was still in force, i.e., Britain could not drop the hot potato until the League approved any changes.[31]

American Interests

In the United States, the State Department was balancing on the diplomatic tight rope. On July 12th, Mr. J. A. Moffett, Chairman of the Board of the Bahrein Petroleum Company (a Standard Oil subsidiary), visited Mr. Wallace Murray, the Under Secretary of State for Near Eastern Affairs. Mr. Moffett told Mr. Murray about the importance of his company's operations in the Persian Gulf region and its concern about Ibn Saud's reaction if there were any U.S. statements in favor of the Jews. There were some disturbing indications that Ibn Saud was leaning towards the British, and there could be serious repercussions (possibly expulsion) if the U.S. angered him. Mr. Moffett was thanked for the information and was told that the U.S. Government was not officially concerned with the present Palestine dispute and had taken no position with respect thereto.[32] England was the mandatory power responsible for Palestine. The American Ambassador in the United Kingdom (Bingham) advised the British Secretary of State (Eden) on August 4th, that America expected to be consulted on any proposed changes to the Mandate which impacted on American interests.[33]

The State Department also monitored the reaction of the Zionist Congress, which met in Zurich on August 11th, and was advised that it had voted 300 to 158 in favor of negotiating with the British on the basis of the Partition Plan.[34] The revisionists had insisted on Jewish "inalienable rights" to all of Palestine and had not given up hopes for Transjordan. The moderates, led by Dr. Chaim Weizmann and David Ben-Gurion were willing to accept the concept. They wanted to negotiate for a larger area in order to have adequate land to reduce the refugee pool in Europe.[35] Although there was wide disagreement among the Jewish groups they met as a group and voted for an overall policy which would be pursued. In unity they had strength.

Arab Disunity

The Arabs had differences of opinion and disunity. The moderate National Defense Party (NDP) had disassociated itself from the Arab Higher Committee on July 3, 1937. The party's President, Raghib

al-Nashashibi, and the ruler of Transjordan, Amir Abdullah, were both
suspected of favoring the partition plan in order to expand their
powers.[36] The NDP wrote the League of Nations and the British Colonial
Secretary and presented its position. The Partition Plan was not
acceptable as proposed because it gave the Jews the best lands and
it subjugated many Arabs to Jewish rule; the Holy Places and many
Arab villages were to be under a permanent Mandate; and the port of
Jaffa would be isolated. As an alternative, the NDP proposed a
democratic state; with minority rights guaranteed; population ratios
fixed as they were; and Jewish land purchases prohibited in the Arab
areas as indicated in the Partition Plan.[37]

The Arab Higher Committee rejected the plan entirely and tried
to dissuade the United States Government from supporting the Jews.
The Mufti of Jerusalem gave the American Consul a note from the Higher
Committee on August 15, 1937. The note was issued in response to
the communications exchanged between the American Ambassador (Bingham)
and Mr. Eden regarding America's right to be consulted on possible
changes to the Mandate. It was observed that the Americans "enjoyed
great respect and affection and a moral standing" in the Arab world,
as well as extensive business connections, both of which were:

> "....worthy of being safeguarded and developed.
> It is our belief that these possess no less pre-
> sent and future value than what the United States
> is likely to reap from supporting the fallacious
> Jewish cause. In fact it exceeds it by far
> inasmuch as it embraces far-flung eastern
> countries."[38]

The American response was very diplomatic. It assured the Mufti
that the position taken was consistent with America's responsibility
toward all of its citizens overseas, and was not based on racial

considerations. The majority of the Americans in Palestine were Jewish, but that did not alter their citizenship nor America's responsibility towards them. The Mufti was "pleased to discover that American action was not unique and designed against the Arabs."[39]

The Arabs probably expected an evasive response from the United States, but they were surprised when they got one from Ibn Saud. When the Royal Commission Report was issued the Arab Higher Committee asked Ibn Saud for his advice on the plan to partition Palestine. His reply was issued on July 13, 1937. It said:

> "The problem of our Arab brethren in Palestine was and still is the subject of our sympathy and our complete concern. You know we did not spare and will never spare anything in our power in order to solve it with justice and fairness with the help of Allah."[40]

This avoidance of the partition plan caused the Arab and Jewish political circles in Jerusalem to wonder if the British were play- ing a game of some sort. The Premier of Iraq (Suleiman) was opposing the plan openly. It was assumed that if the British were serious about the plan Iraq would be quiet, not Saudi Arabia.[41] There was one man who was considered close to Ibn Saud who was not quiet.

St. John Philby published an opinion and recommendations in the September issue of The Contemporary Review, London, 1937. He opened his article with the observation that the Jews were willing to negotiate and the Arabs were - "astonished at the concession of ninetenths of their extremist demands, demand the whole pound of flesh promised by McMahon." He continued - "the friends of the Arabs [i.e., Philby]* counsel acceptance...subject to the discussion of

*my comment

details. To their friends they turn a deaf ear, pleading religious scruples to the recognition of a Jewish State in Arab territory."[42] Philby argued that although Jews existed in peace in other Arab territories such as Yemen, Iraq, Syria and Saudi Arabia; Palestine was different. Since the days of Moses there was conflict between Jews and Gentiles, and therefore partition or rule by a neutral power was required. As Philby saw it:

> "Partition can scarcely be other than temporary,
> for that alone can compel the two parties to
> an agreed settlement on the basis of Arab
> sovereighty and Jewish privilege. From such
> a settlement both parties have everything to
> gain. Only the Jews can profit by the
> continuance of the existing Mandatory administra-
> tion."[43]

What Philby seems to imply is that neither state would be economically viable and that they would have to negotiate to achieve mutual benefits. He addressed the particulars of his proposed changes to the Partition plan only after he dropped a bombshell on the Arabs.

As he saw the issues, an understanding between the Arabs and Jews was feasible and had been partially attempted by Nashashibi (NDP leader). However, the real issue was "the old factor of Arab internal discord."[44] The Partition plan would give Abdullah of Transjordan a throne and control over a significantly greater territory than he had. Philby alluded to the old animosity between Abdullah and Ibn Saud, "the only Arabian King that matters." The Mufti too, according to Philby, was obviously opposed to Abdullah's benefitting from the plan. And so it seemed, Arab rivalry (particularly Saudi vs. Hashimite) precluded an agreement, or even negotiations along the lines proposed by the Commission. Philby followed up his chastisement of Arab discord with some recommendations.

Either Abdullah must step aside and give up his dream or the rest of the Arabs must acquiesce. Philby believed that a round table conference could be convened to determine the outcome for Arab Palestine on the basis of the Partition plan. If the Arabs reached an agreement it would command attention and respect from the British and the League of Nations. Philby proposed that the Arabs start with the Partition plan as a basis for negotiations. The Jews wanted the Negeb (Negev) desert for development, but they certainly did not want the 225,000 Arabs in northern Palestine. And those Arabs did not want to be under Jewish rule. Philby added - "the suggestion of their voluntary or forced removal from their ancestral territories is too fantastic to require examination."[45] (This point has to be kept in mind for future consideration). Philby's argument for modifications of the Partition plan can be summarized as six issues:

1. The Arab tract of northern Palestine down to Acre on the coast should be reunited with Syria.

2. Acre should not be developed in rivarly to Haifa by Syria and Tel-Aviv's development should be abandoned in the interest of Jaffa. Thus the Arabs and Jews would each have a Palestinian port and there would be no need for Mandatory control of Jaffa.

3. With no Mandatory of Jaffa there would be no need for a corridor and the area designated as a corridor should be divided between the Arabs and the Jews.

4. The area around Rehovoth is significant to the Jews (Agricultural research center and home of Dr. Weizmann) and should

either be exchanged for an equally productive area contigous to the Jewish zone or kept as a detached enclave. There could be no corridor, as they in Philby's view were unworkable. The link between the two areas would have to be by sea.

5. The Commission's proposal for a sacred enclave for Jerusalem and Bethlehem was valid. However, the League of Nations should release the British from the requirement and establish an international commission to administer the enclave. An international police force such as that used in Shanghi or Tangiers should keep the peace. External powers such as the League, the United States and the Governments of Arabia would guarantee the enclave's neutrality.

6. Aqabah rightly belonged to Saudi Arabia. If Britain could not concede it to Ibn Saud, it should at least be under Palestinian Arab control.

Recognizing the Jewish sentiment toward Jerusalem, Philby argued that that "dream" would have to be surrendered if Jews wanted to expand and develop. What he implied was that Arabs would accept Jewish economic expansion into Arab lands (to include Transjordan) if they came as guests.

Philby then pointed to the Arabs and assessed their attitude.

> "To them [the Arabs] the creation of a Jewish State in a tiny fraction of Palestine seems infinitely worse than the abandonment of the whole country to foreign domination."46

Compromise was necessary and inevitable in Philby's view. He offered the Arabs the fact that they could have full sovereignty over four-fifths of the area, while the Jews would be segregated in one-fifth of the land. The land was the Arab's negotiating lever. He warned

that if the Arabs did not accept the principles of the Partition
plan--and the Mandatory was left in control, the Jews would
inevitably become the majority population in Palestine.

The perceptiveness displayed by Philby was really quite striking.
However, his lack of tact greatly reduced the effectiveness of his
arguments. The Arabs, and especially Ibn Saud, wasted no time in
expressing their displeasure with his exposure of their dirty
laundry. Philby had had similar articles in the London newspapers
earlier and Ibn Saud had informed them in July that his dealings
with Philby were purely personal and commercial.

> "Some may think that Philby's opinions reflect
> our own....As for his personal opinions, they
> are his own and do not reflect our thoughts
> at all."47

Philby published his confirmation shortly thereafter:

> "I want to make clear that I agree with all
> that has been publicly stated by the Saudi
> Arabian Embassy about me, and that I have
> never in the whole of the last twenty years
> (1917-1937)* expressed any but my personal
> opinion. I am pleased to have this oppor-
> tunity to affirm that neither now nor in
> the past have I had any official or semi-
> official connection of any kind with His
> Majesty; my admiration for him is another
> matter."48

What Philby failed to remember was his attempt to mediate between
Ibn Saud and Sherif Ali in 1924, just before Ibn Saud took over the
Hijaz. Philby was informed in a letter at that time that:

> "If there is something personal you are
> welcome to discuss it with me personally.
> If however there is something that pertains
> to the Hijaz and you wish to act as a
> mediator, I would suggest your holding
> aloof from it. As you will observe, it is
> a purely Islamic problem in which your
> mediation will be uncalled for."49

*inserted by me

Philby was never one to stay aloof if he believed he had something
to say. He did however know how to adjust his opinion according
to the circumstances of the moment.

Philby published another article in the October 1937 issue of
Foreign Affairs. It was entitled "The Arabs and the Future of
Palestine."[50] He began his article with a short history of the
relationship between the British and the Arabs since 1913; the Hussein-
McMahon correspondence; the Sykes-Picot Agreement; and the imposition
of the Mandates. He described the recovery of Arab independence in
Iraq and the favorable prospects for Syria, which left only
Palestine and Transjordan under an indefinite Mandate control. The
problem though (as Philby saw it) was that the Mandate "was framed
mainly to realize the nationalist ideals of Zionism." And that was
why the Mandate was unworkable. Philby applauded the Royal
Commission's efforts and its call for Partition. There was only one
alternative to Partition - the annexation of Palestine as a Crown
Colony of the British Empire.[51] Philby was obviously trying to get
the Arab's attention and show them what could result from their
intransigence.

In assessing the reason for Arab intransigence, Philby said
nothing about internal discord. His opinion was that:

> "the root-and-branch opposition of the
> Palestine Arabs and their supporters can
> only be regarded as manouvering for posi-
> tion. The Arabs are bad bargainers. In
> this case nine-tenths of their full demands
> have been conceded. They reject the con-
> cession in the hope of getting ten-tenths.
> It is inconceivable that they should get
> that. It is conceivable that they may lose
> what is now offered."[52]

Again he called upon the Arabs to accept the Partition as a basis for furter negotiations.

In the remainder of his October article he proposed the same modifications to the Royal Commission's Partition plan, except for two key points. He envisioned the Arab portion of Palestine being united with Syria.[53] Philby did not present his rationale so I will offer a possibility. The probability of Ibn Saud obtaining control did not seem to be too great; and there was obvious opposition from Ibn Saud to a Hashemite getting it; the next alternative for Arab control had to be Syria. The other key point pertained to the form of guarantee for the Partition and peace.

The Jews were not expected to rely upon the Arab promises, and it was realized that the British had regional interests that required protection. What Philby offered was the idea that the Jews would certainly be within their rights to negotiate with the British Government for a British garrison on Jewish soil.[54] Thus everyone would receive something they could live with. Philby stated that it was up to the Arabs to show statesmanship, and he believed that they would surely accept.[55] Philby was adjusting his position hoping that he could persuade the Arabs that they had to negotiate. Unfortunately, the Palestinian Arab extremists were making negotiations difficult.

As mentioned earlier, the Arab Higher Committee in Jerusalem had rejected the Partition plan. By January 1938 the Higher Committee was declared illegal by the Palestine (Mandatory) Government, and was in exile in Damascus, Syria. The Mufti published a manifesto which opposed the Partition plan and the British intention to send another commission for further investigation. According to the Mufti the Arabs demanded:

> "1. Full independence for Palestine Arabs.
> 2. A definite end to the British experiment for a Jewish National Home.
> 3. Termination of the British Mandate, with a treaty similar to that between Britain and Iraq.
> 4. Complete stoppage of Jewish immigration and prohibition of the sale of land to Jews."[56]

It was further declared that the Arabs were willing to negotiate to secure "reasonable interests of Britain" and for the protection of the Holy Places, including the legal rights of the Jews. However, no Arab was going to negotiate with the British Commission. And so, a substantial road block had been erected. Undaunted, Philby proposed yet another solution.

While enroute back to Saudi Arabia he stopped in Cairo and issued his fourth proposal. The Commission should defer its trip for six months while the Arabs conferred in Jedda, under the auspices of Ibn Saud. The exiled Higher Committee leaders such as Haj Amin el Husseni (the Mufti of Jerusalem) should be granted amnesty and participate in the Arab conference. Once all possiblities were explored, and an Arab consensus establishad, the Jewish leaders should be invited to Jedda for talks. If an agreement were reached then Partition would not be necessary (that should entice the Mufti), and if negotiations failed Partition was still available as a solution. The Arabs press in Cairo endorsed Philby's proposal but the Jews and the British did not seem to pay much attention to it.[57] There were at this time numerous proposals presented - and the moderate Jewish leaders indicated a willingness to meet with Arab leaders - but they never did.[58] Philby had accurately identified the problem in his September

1937 article - internal Arab discord made negotiations imposs ble.

Ibn Saud Gets Involved

Throughout 1938 the Arabs suffered from infighting while the Jews tried to strengthen their positions. When the British realized that nothing was being accomplished in Palestine, they announced in a White Paper (November 9, 1938) that they were calling the Arab and Jewish representatives to London to confer on a solution. Immediately the various factions began jockeying for position.[59] King Ibn Saud sought the support of the United States by sending a lengthy letter (Appendix E) to President F. D. Roosevelt (November 29, 1938). He provided the President with an historical account of the Arab and Jewish positions in Palestine, a review of the contradictory promises made by the British, and the establishment of the Mandate. He referred President Roosevelt to the findings of the 1919 King-Crane Commission which President Wilson had sponsored. If the President reviewed that Commission's findings he would appreciate the Arab position. Palestine had received more than its fair share of Jews. It was time some other countries opened their doors too.[60]

President Roosevelt replied on January 17, 1939. His very brief note advised Ibn Saud that America would maintain a consistent policy as it had all along. American interests, spiritual and economic, would be protected in accordance with the provisions of the American-British Mandate Convention of December 3, 1924.[61] I interpret that as saying that the official position was that Britain was responsible for the Mandate and America was neutral, unless U.S. interests were endangered. Ibn Saud had not gained an ally, but then he did not have a major opponent either.

Prior to receiving the President's reply, Ibn Saud authorized Philby to publish an interview he had given him earlier. The article was published in London, Milan and New York in December 1938, just prior to the forthcoming Arab-Jewish-British conference in London (Appendix F). It is obvious that Philby was trying to get Ibn Saud to expound on the Palestine problem, but the King was hesitant because of his respect for Britain's position. He believed that the British, if they considered the problem with their own and Arab interests in mind, would choose a reasonable course. If not, there was nothing he could say to change their minds. Philby asked what advice the King had for the Arabs. Ibn Saud's reply was that they should be unified in the pursuit of their objectives. The King regretted that they were not unified. (In so doing, he confirmed Philby's September article on Palestine). As he observed the multiple factions in disagreement, he decided to step back from the issue and express himself only to those who asked him questions on Arabia or Islam. When Philby asked the King about the Balfour declaration, the King exclaimed "The Balfour promise was indeed the greatest injustice of Great Britain." As for the possibility of a Jewish State - even if all the other Arabs recognized it - Ibn Saud would not. He said it would not be consistent with his religion or in the interests of his situation.[62]

Ibn Saud dispatched his son, Emir Faisal, and Fuad Bey Hamza as his representatives to the Palestine Round Table Conference in January 1939. Also, asked to "be on hand" was St. John Philby.[63] It is evident from this fact that Ibn Saud must have considered Philby as an asset. If he were considered as a possibly disruptive or counter-productive agent he surely would not have been invited. Of course there is the possibility that the Saudi delegation might benefit from having an "unofficial" Englishman who could make contacts with either the British or the Jews. If his activities became known to opponents, the Saudis could disavow him. He did have a clandestine meeting with the Jewish leaders - Dr. Weizmann and Ben-Gurion. They came to his house to meet with Fuad Hamza. As Philby recorded the meeting: he proposed that Emir Faisal should become the King of Palestine and that there by a quid pro quo on Jewish immigration, to the extent of 50,000 in five years.[64] Nothing came of that plan either. The whole Round Table Conference was a failure.

The Conference opened on February 7, 1939 at St. James Palace. It was obvious from the start that negotiations were going to be difficult. The Arabs refused to meet with the Jews face to face. The British had to do what would in later years be called "shuttle diplomacy", but it was done in London in the same building. The British presented three different proposals and none were accepted. On March 17, 1939 the Conference was terminated. And as the British had stated, they dictated the policy to be pursued since the Arabs and Jews refused to reach an agreement.[65]

The British White Paper, 1939

The British White Paper on Palestine was issued on May 17, 1939. It reported that the Arabs and Jews had had an opportunity to reach an agreement but failed. As a result of the Conference it was appreciated that the concept of a Jewish National Home in Palestine was valid, but there was a limit to immigration which would not be exceeded. In reference to the Arab claims that the Hussein-McMahon correspondence included Palestine, that was denied. Meetings had been held to clarify the language of that correspondence, and it was determined that the area west of the Jordan was excluded from Arab independence. It was regretable that there was a misunderstanding.[67] As to the policy to be enacted, the White Paper stated that the British objective was to see an independent Palestinian State in 10 years.

In order to achieve that objective there was to be a transition from British to indigenous control once there was peace. The White Paper addressed the three major concerns of the two groups and stipulated how they were to be controlled.

1) Constitution. The Arabs and Jews would share in the governing of the State. As peace was established, they would be integrated into governmental positions. Five years after peace was restored a Constitution would be written by a representative body with Arabs, Jews and British participation. The interests of all concerned were to be embodied in and protected by the provisions of the Constitution.

2) Immigration. The concept of economic absorptive capacity was valid only to a finite point. Therefore, starting April 1, 1939 there would be controlled immigration for five years, with a total of 75,000 Jews admitted. That would result in one-third of the population being Jewish. After that limit was reached, further immigration would be dependent upon Arab acquiescence. The number of illegal immigrants would be counted against the total number authorized.

3) Land. A High Commissioner was to be empowered to prohibit and regulate land transfer to protect the interests of peace. The

British wanted the Arabs and Jews to work out their differences and find peace together; the British had a bigger conflict in Europe to worry about.

Philby Develops His "Plan"

As World War II broke out in Europe, St. John Philby assumed an anti-war posture. He joined the British People's Party and ran for Parliament. He lost receiving 576 of 22,169 votes.[68] Not deterred by this defeat, he continued his anti-war speeches and called for a recognition of "Germany as a principle factor in the shape of things to come."[69] He tried to get a government job as an Arabist, but was not accepted. Since he could not work for the British government, he decided to work for Ibn Saud. And so we come to Philby's final plan for the solution to the Palestine problem.

Philby wrote about his "plan" in his book Arabian Jubilee (1953). In presenting the background of the problem he presents the view that the European Jew and Judaism had "always been regarded in Islam with feelings akin to contempt..."[70] His contention was that if a real leader had declared a Jihad when the Jewish National Home project started, it would have been "stifled at birth."[71] Unfortunately, Ibn Saud had not yet established himself in 1920. However, by 1933 Ibn Saud was powerful and respected. Philby believed that Ibn Saud was the only Arab leader who could secure a general acceptance of a formula for peace - Philby's formula.

Philby wrote that his view of the situation in 1939 was based on expediency and not the merits of the case. In his opinion the European Jews had no legal or moral right to go to Palestine.[72]

However, the fact of the matter was that the Jews were in Palestine
and Britain was going to protect them. When Britain realized the
errors of the Mandate, Philby (as has been presented above) tried
to get the Arabs to negotiate. He realized that the War would
seriously restrict the Pilgrimage and Ibn Saud would be short of the
funds he needed to keep his country going. Oil had been found in
1938, but its shipment and the royalties would be greatly reduced
until the war was over and tankers could travel freely.[73] Philby
devised a plan which he believed would satisfy the needs of all
parties.

Once again Philby met with the Zionist leaders at the Athenaeum
Club (September 28, 1939). During a lunch with Dr. Chaim Weizmann,
Professor Lewis Namier, Professor of Modern History in the University
of Manchester, and Philby proposed his plan:

> "The whole of Palestine should be left to
> the Jews. All Arabs displaced therefrom
> should be resettled elsewhere at the expense
> of the Jews, who would place a sum of £20
> millions at the disposal of King Ibn Saud
> for this purpose. All other Asiatic Arab
> countries, with the sole exception of Aden
> should be formally recognized as completely
> independent in the proper sense of the
> term."[74]

The plan was to be proposed to Ibn Saud by Britain and America, and
if accepted the two powers were to guarantee support.[75] Philby's
record indicates that the Jewish leadership approved his plan on
October 6, 1939.[76] Dr. Weizmann was to contact the British and
American Governments and Philby was to inform Ibn Saud of the forthcoming official proposal.

Professor Namier's memorandum (Appendix G) on the meeting

indicates that the form of payment would have to be in Jewish

goods:

> "e.g., if Ibn Saud requires arms - and this
> was one of the main items talked of by Philby -
> we could, over a certain period of time,
> supply them from Jewish armament works in
> Palestine."[77]

The Arabist and the Zionists had no difficulty reaching an agreement

on Philby's plan. The next step was to present it to their benefactors.

Chapter Two Notes

1. P.R.C.F.O./371/16878. E3745/3745/25 Jedda to London, June 19, 1933, p. 27.

2. H. St. John Philby. Arabian Days: An Autobiography (London: Robert Hale Lim., 1948), p. 283.

3. Esco Foundation for Palestine Inc. Palestine: A Study of Jewish, Arab, and British Policies (New Haven: Yale University Press, 1947), p. 674.

4. J. C. Hurewitz. The Struggle for Palestine. (New York: Green Wood Press, 1968), p. 68.

5. Ibid., p. 68.

6. David Ben-Gurion. My Talks with Arab Leaders. (Jerusalem: Ketter Books, 1972), pp. 121-141.

7. Ibid., p. 123.

8. Ibid., p. 124.

9. Ibid., p. 126. "Eretz Israel" means literally "land of Israel" In 1951 Mr. Begin recalled that he had always been taught it was regarded "since Biblical times as the motherland of the children of Israel. It has always comprised what came subsequently to be called Palestine on both sides of the River Jordan, i.e., not only the present State of Israel (8100 square miles) in Western Palestine (10,429 square miles), but also Transjordan (34,700 square miles), once the habitat of the Hebrew tribes of Reuben, Gad and the half-tribe Menasseh." Menachem Begin. The Revolt: Story of the Irgun (New York: Henry Schuman, 1951), p. 3. Note.

10. Monroe., p. 196.

11. Ben-Gurion, Talks., p. 128.

12. Ibid., p. 129.

13. Ibid., p. 131. See also: Ben-Gurion's Letters to Paula. (Pittsburg: University of Pittsburg Press, 1972), p. 116.

14. Ben-Gurion. Talks., p. 133.

15. H. C. Armstrong. Lord of Arabia (London: Baker, 1934).

16. Ben-Gurion. Talks., p. 127.

17. Ibid., p. 134.

18. Ibid.

19. Ibid., pp. 140-141.

20. Ibid., p. 137.

21. Ibid., p. 139.

22. Ibid.

23. Ibid., p. 140.

24. Hurewitz. Struggle., p. 72.

25. Great Britain, Parliamentary Papers, 1936-37, Command Paper (Cmd) 5479.

26. Hurewitz. Struggle., p. 73.

27. Ibid.

28. Ibid., p. 74.

29. Ibid., p. 76.

30. Great Britain, Parliamentary Papers, July 1937, Command Paper (Cmd) 5513.

31. Hurewitz. Struggle., p. 77.

32. United States Department of State, Foreign Relations of the United States (Hereafter FRUS), 1937, II, p. 893.

33. Ibid., p. 901.

34. Ibid., p. 904. Hurewitz, Struggle, indicates the vote was 298-160.

35. Hurewitz. Struggle., p. 77.

36. Ibid., p. 78.

37. Ibid., p. 79.

38. FRUS, 1937, II, p. 905.

39. Ibid.

40. New York Times, July 14, 1937, p 11.

41. Ibid.

42. The Contemporary Review, September 1937, Vol. 153, No. 861, p. 265.

43. Ibid.

44. Ibid., p. 266.

45. Ibid.

46. Ibid., p. 269.

47. Monroe., p. 214.

48. Ibid., p. 215.

49. Ibid., p. 143.

50. Foreign Affairs, October 1937, pp. 156-166.

51. Ibid., p. 161.

52. Ibid., p. 162.

53. Ibid., p. 164.

54. Ibid., p. 165.

55. Ibid., p. 166.

56. New York Times, January 16, 1938, p. 31.

57. Ibid.

58. ESCO Foundation for Palestine, Inc. <u>Palestine: A Study of Jewish, Arab, and British Policies</u>. New Haven, 1947, pp. 881-886.

59. Ibid., pp. 887-889.

60. FRUS, 1938, I, p. 994

61. FRUS, 1939, IV, p. 696.

62. H. St. John Philby, "King Ibn Saud Speaks At Last". <u>Asia</u>, December 1938, p. 718.

63. Monroe, p. 219.

64. Ibid.

65. ESCO, pp. 891-900.

66. J. C. Hurewitz. <u>Diplomacy in the Near and Middle East. A Documentary Record: 1914-1956</u>. New York, 1956, pp. 218-226.

67. Great Britain, Parliamentary Papers, Command Paper (Cmd) 5974. See also Elie Kedouri, <u>In the Anglo-Arab Labyrinth: The McMahon-Husayn Correspondence and its Interpretations 1941-1939.</u>, (London: Cambridge University Press, 1976).

68. Monroe, p. 220.

69. Ibid.

70. H. St. John Philby. <u>Arabian Jubilee</u>. (New York: John Day Co., 1953), p. 205.

71. Ibid.

72. Ibid., p. 209.

73. Monroe, p. 221.

74. Philby. <u>Jubilee</u>, pp. 212-213.

75. Ibid.

76. Philby's papers, St. Anthony's College, Oxford. Box X, File 3.

77. Ibid.

CHAPTER THREE

PHILBY, IBN SAUD AND PALESTINE, 1940-1945:

WHAT HAPPENED WITH PHILBY'S PLAN?

St. John Philby developed a plan to solve the Palestine
problem and the Zionist leadership approved it. But, the problem
was not resolved. The question which naturally comes to mind is:
what happened to Philby's plan? The short answer is that it was
buried in the rubble created by conflicting interest groups and
personalities during the period 1940-1945. This chapter will
provide a more comprehensive reconstruction of what happened.

Dr. Weizmann and the British

In October 1939, Dr. Chaim Weizmann, President of the World
Zionist Organization, discussed the Palestine problem and a
possible solution to it with Brenden Bracken, Parliamentary Private
Secretary for Winston Churchill. At that time Mr. Churchill was
First Lord of the Admiralty and Mr. Bracken was one of his closest
aides. On 31 October 1939 Mr. Bracken wrote a memorandum to
Mr. Churchill regarding his discussion with Dr. Weizmann. He
stated "I have great sympathy with the Zionists, but I am
completely ignorant about Palestine,"... however he then added
that "Palestine could obviously flourish as a Jewish State."
He asked Mr. Churchill:

"Have you ever considered the idea of sub-
sidising the Arabs to leave Palestine?
Hitler's scheme for decanting German
minorities is not without merit. You will
remember what Max told you about President
Roosevelt's anxiety about finding a home
for the persecuted Jews. I imagine he
would very willingly foster and help to
finance a scheme to provide an alternative
(and incidently better) home for the
Palestinian Arabs. Palestine can then
provide a home for several million Jews.
Weizmann was very much attracted by this
idea, and has discussed it with one of
the leading Arab representatives. He has
just told me that the Emir of Trans-Jordan*
has stated that in return for a subsidy of
20 million pounds he will offer Arabs a
much better home than they have ever had
in Palestine.+

I know this is a daring, not to say mad,
scheme but we live in such an ill-contrived
world that it might well work."

+This subsidy will be provided by Americans.[1]

[*my emphasis]

It is impossible to confirm (at this time) whether Mr. Bracken

mistakenly referred to the Emir of Transjordan as the Arab Leader

Dr. Weizmann talked to, or not. Also, we do not know if the

reference to "Americans" paying the 20 million pounds meant Jewish

Americans, American donations or the American Government. It is

interesting to note that a man of his influence admits complete

ignorance about Palestine and yet is confident of its potential as a

Jewish State. Mr. Churchill's immediate response is not known, but,

as it will be showr below, he discussed the matter with Dr.

Weizmann at a later date.

Philby and Ibn Saud

St. John Philby returned to Saudi Arabia and so on 8 January

1940 presented to Ibn Saud the plan for solving the Palestine problem.
Ibn Saud did not reject Philby's proposed solution. Philby recorded
that the King told him:

> that some such arrangement might be possible in
> appropriate future circumstances, that he would
> keep the matter in mind, that he would give me
> a definite answer at the appropriate time, that
> meanwhile I should not breathe a word about the
> matter to anyone - least of all to any Arab and,
> finally, that if the proposals became the sub-
> ject of public discussion with any suggestion of
> his approving them he would have no hesitation
> whatsoever in denouncing me as having no authority
> to commit him in the matter.[2]

Ibn Saud had to look at Philby's plan from his position as the
ruler of Saudi Arabia. He was the King/Imam of a newly created
theocratic state which was politically, but not yet financially,
independent. As protector of the Holy Cities of Mecca and Medina
he also had to be mindful of the entire Moslem world's interests in
Palestine, e.g., the Moslem inhabitants and the Islamic holy places.
Ibn Saud had consistently demonstrated to the British a willingness
to find a moderate solution in Palestine and was in fact opposed
to the extremist actions of the Mufti of Jerusalem.[3] Ibn Saud was
also very concerned about the expansion of Hashimite power in the
region. Of particular concern was the possibility that Syria might
be joined with either Hasimite Kingdom of Transjordan or Iraq and
thereby make a Hashimite ruler powerful enough to threaten the Hijaz
or the Najd.[4] This rivalry between the two Houses complicated all
efforts among the Arabs in search of a solution for the Palestine
problem. The outbreak of World War II in September of 1939 introduced
another major impediment in the search for a solution.

Ibn Saud secretly notified the British on September 3, 1939

that, "he would never give any undertaking or take any secret or open action with any Moslem or (other) foreign government which might damage British interests or affect his relations with His Majesty's Government."[5]

By avoiding public declarations in favor of either side, Ibn Saud was able to protect his political and economic interests as well as those of the British. Saudi Arabia could not contribute any significant fighting force to oppose the Italian Fascists in Ethiopia or North Africa; but Ibn Saud could suppress anti-British agitation within his country and be a moderating influence in the Moslem world. The British were grateful and evaluated Ibn Saud's position as "benevolent neutrality;" "he hated Hitler as a disturber of the peace. and the Soviet regime as a menace to Islam."[6] It is probable that Ibn Saud was also mindful of the prospect that the War would reduce the flow of pilgrims to Mecca and the export of oil, thus making his financial dependence on Britain more pronounced.

With the above factors in mind, Ibn Saud's reaction to Philby's proposal may be evaluated. Ibn Saud could gain a great deal from the implementation of such a plan. If the Jews were to be allotted the whole of Palestine west of the Jordan river and the Palestinian Arabs, under his suzerainty, transferred elsewhere at Jewish expense, Ibn Saud would have to control that 'elsewhere'. The envisioned 'elsewhere' was Transjordan and Iraq. His suzerainty could be established if the British withdrew their support from the Hashimites. In 1939 Ibn Saud told the British that their power was the only reason Hussein's heirs were rulers. He added that he had no expansionist ambitions toward Iraq, Transjordan or Syria. He believed that the

will of the people should prevail.[7] It is, however, unlikely that
he would have rejected suzerainty if the British offered it. He
would then be in a position to grant independence if the people in
the region did not want him as their ruler.[8] In either case the
Hashimites would be out of power.

The major difficulty with Philby's plan was that Ibn Saud would
have to concede to the establishment of a Jewish State. As the
Imam of an Islamic, fundamentalist, theocratic state, Ibn Saud would
require an irrefutable rationale in order to gain the support of his
Ulema. In 1938 he had already stated in an interview published by
Philby: "that such action would not be consistent with my religion
nor would it be to the interests of the situation in which I find
myself."[9]

Ibn Saud's religious views would never change, but the situation
was changing. In 1939 the British had issued their White Paper, but
they were not very scucessful in stemming the flow of Jewish
immigrants. By the end of that year nearly 30,000 Jews had entered
Palestine.[10] Axis propaganda spoke of British plans to establish
a Zionist state in Palestine.[11] The British had previously demonstrated
their commitment to the Zionist portion of the Balfour declaration,
and the Zionists were still very adamant about their objectives.[12]
If a Jewish state seemed inevitable, Philby's plan might represent
the least disastrous solution. At least the Jews would be made to
pay for the land and finance the displaced Arabs in new territory.
The alternative would be war.

The King had thus far maintained a moderate policy toward Palestine
in support of the British promises for a just solution. On 2 December

1939, Sir Reader Bullard, prior to his departure from Jedda to his new post in Tehran, submitted his final report on Ibn Saud.

> "On the whole he has shown himself a great
> ruler. No man who had not had a firm hold
> over himself as well as over his people
> could have steered the course in regard to
> Palestine which he has steered for the last
> two or three years. It is not that he is
> cynical: the depths of his personal feel-
> ings could not be doubted by anyone who had
> heard him repeat some of the Quranic texts
> about the Jews or seen him trying to suppress
> his tears at the wireless announcement of
> the hanging of an Arab for participation in
> the armed movement in Palestine; but he is
> not led away by his feelings but keeps his
> eyes fixed steadfastly on the main lines of
> the policy which he has adopted. I do not
> think that the possession of a certain great-
> ness of mind can be denied him."[13]

Ibn Saud's reaction to Philby's proposal was totally consistent with the philosophy he professed in his earlier interview. The King maintained faith in the words of the poet:

> "Wisdom consists of acting only when the
> consequences of your act you clearly ken.*"[14]
> (*ken: to have sight of; discern)

Before the King would enter any situation he would always make sure that he also had an exit. If there was anything to Philby's proposal, all Ibn Saud had to do was wait for the Americans and the British to come forward with the proposal.

In March Philby asked him to commit himself regarding the proposition. Ibn Saud had not been approached by the British so he told Philby that he found it difficult to collaborate with him.[15] There is evidence that in April 1940 Ibn Saud tested the British to determine whether or not they were thinking along the same lines as Philby represented them to be. He sent a message to the British

Foreign Minister concerning the growing problem of Palestinian refugees. He said that Nari Pasha, the Prime Minister of Iraq, had approached him and wanted the neighboring Arab states to agree on some means of solving the problem. Ibn Saud wanted the British to know that:

> "personally he would prefer to leave the matter entirely in the hands of His Majesty's Government and Palestine authorities whom it primarily concerned but as a friend he felt obliged to point out that these refugees formed a dangerous nucleus of anti-British feeling and as an Arab rule⁻ he would probably be unable to disassociate himself from the action proposed by Iraq and Egypt."16

If the British government supported Philby's plan, Ibn Saud had just presented them with a prime opportunity to broach the subject. They did not. It seems that in 1940, only two members of the British government knew of Philby's plan: Brenden Bracken and Winston Churchill.

The British Foreign Office was, however, very much concerned with Philby. Stonehewer-Bird, the new British Minister in Jedda, clearly expressed his perception of Philby in his February 1940 report to London:

> "Among the less desirable British Moslems who performed the pilgrimage this year must be classed Haji Abdullah Philby. His defeatist attitude, his criticism of His Majesty's Government for entering on "an unncessary war which was ruining Arabia," the scorn which he poured on the British news service, his accusation that figures of British shipping losses were deliberately falsified disgusted the legation and the British community and drove the French Minister to protest to His Majesty's Minister and to send a strongly worded telegram to the French Government. Philby is unrepentant, he is ready to admit that if he were a

> German acting in this manner in war-time
> he would long since have been shot, but he
> is an Englishman entitled to free speech.
> He is the only man who knows the truth
> and has the courage to tell it. His
> influence with Ibn Saud is in the opinion
> of this legation most negligible, the
> King's counsellors hate him, the average
> Arab dislikes and despises him for his
> apostasy, but His Majesty's Minister
> nevertheless shares his French colleagues
> view that it is highly improper if not
> actually dangerous for him to talk as
> he does in mixed company of Syrians,
> Indians, Iraqis, Egyptians and Americans.
> A full report comprising a selection of
> Mr. Philby's more offensive utterances
> has been furnished to the Foreign Office
> in London."[17]

Stonehewer-Bird reported Philby's "offensive utterances" to London

on February 12, 1940. Subsequently numerous messages were exchanged

between the Foreign Office, the India Office, the Middle East

Intelligence Center, and the Ministers in Cairo, Khartoum and

Jedda. The main focus of all the messages was what to do about

Philby. To ask Ibn Saud to throw him out would imply a lack of faith

in the King's judgement. Threaten him with suspension of his

pension? No, there were insufficient grounds to do that. By June it

was determined that the only thing that could be done was wait for

him to return to England, and then hold his passport.[18] To the

British, Philby was a "political menace" whose presence was "a thorn

in the flesh."

According to Hafez Wahba, Foreign Minister in Jedda, "the King

liked Philby (he is certainly Ibn Saud's best publicity agent) but

laughed at his opinions." Hafez told Philby that "the only affect

of his disloyalty to England was to arouse suspicion in the minds of

his listeners that his anti-British talk was a cloak for pro-British

activities."[19] Philby probably added credence to such suspicions
when in May he approached two of Ibn Saud's secretaries with his
plan for Palestine in the guise of an "academic proposition."
Philby expected some hostility but he also believed they would keep
their discussions confidential.[20] One was a Syrian and the other
was a Palestinian. Naturally Ibn Saud heard of Philby's talk and
summoned him immediately. The King rebuked Philby for disregarding
his warning and told him not to repeat the error. Ibn Saud was still
not willing to commit himself on the plan and Philby was again told
to wait.[21] In June 1940, the King, desirins to make Philby's waiting
pleasant, gave him a new house in Riyadh. Thus Philby would be
away from the European community in Jedda and under the watchful
eye of Ibn Saud. That may have been Ibn Saud's intent but Philby
did not stay in Riyadh long.

In mid-June 1940, Philby decided that he wanted to leave Arabia
and go to America. Why he wanted to go is an interesting but
incomplete puzzle. Philby cabled Weizmann in Washington D.C. on
February 2nd, that he was "progressing slowly."[22] Weizmann was
visiting America and tentatively broached Philby's plan to the State
Department and had a "theoretical" discussion with President
Roosevelt.[23] Returning to England in March Weizmann planned
to make another trip to America in May, but that had to be
indefinitely postponed due to the military situation.[24] In mid-
April, Philby's wife, Dora, relayed a status report to Weizmann:

> "Ibn Saud...still won't say yes and won't say
> no. The truth is that he himself is quite
> favorably inclined towards the proposal and
> is just thinking out how it can be worked
> without producing a howl of anger among cer-
> tain Arab elements....Dr. W. can go on with
> his idea and work up the American side of
> the scheme but we may have to wait for a bit
> for a favorable opportunity of putting it
> into practice. Of course he (Ibn Saud)
> doesn't want to be accused of sacrificing
> Arab interests to his own ambitions...."[25]

But Weizmann was stuck in England and could not go to America.

According to Philby, "It was entirely on my own initiative that I

decided.....to leave Arabia for America."[26] He gave the King the

feeble excuse that he wanted to go because communications with his

family were cut off. Ibn Saud directed his Minister in London to

send weekly bulletins about Philby's family. Philby, however,

insisted that he must go, disregarding the King's warning that he

could not protect him outside Arabia.

Ibn Saud notified Stonehewer-Bird in Jedda of Philby's intentions.

He asked the British Minister to facilitate Philby's journey. The

Minister's telegram to London on July 12, 1940, reported that:

> "Philby was, the King thought, mentally de-
> ranged; he never ceased heaping curses and
> insults and scorn on the British Government.
> He had told Ibn Saud that he wished to travel
> to India and the United States of America
> for the purpose of conducting anti-British
> propaganda. Ibn Saud has given orders to
> the Saudi authorities to keep close watch
> on him pending his departure and to inform
> him that if he indulges in anti-British talk
> he will be imprisoned."[27]

The tenor of the above text is extremely derogatory toward Philby.

Did Philby actually tell Ibn Saud that he was going to America to

defame the King's benefactor? That is unlikely. Was Ibn Saud's

Arabic misrepresented? Stonehewer-Bird certainly did not like Philby, but he had nothing to gain from such a report. Errors in translation between an Arab King and a British Minister had occurred before, but the meaning of this message was not dependent on one word.[28] The message makes sense if its intent was to stop Philby from getting to America. If Philby could not keep his plan to himself in Saudi Arabia, he would probably try to pursue it in America (even if that were not his main reason for going). Ibn Saud was a ruler who wanted to protect his interests. Regardless of his intentions, a tactless Philby loose in America might do Ibn Saud more harm than good.

Philby never made it to America. The British monitored his every move. That was not difficult for he had submitted his itinerary and request for visas to them.[29] He left Jedda for Bahrain on July 17th. When he arrived on July 29th, his luggage was searched for possible evidence of anti-British propaganda. Nothing was found and Philby was amused by the incident.[30] Philby sailed for Karachi four days later. The British Political Agent in Bahrain telegraphed Philby's expected arrival date to the Secretary of State for India and included the observation: "His behaviour here was harmless."[31] Intending to keep him harmless for as long as possible the British arrested Philby upon his arrival in Karachi and then sent him to England on the next ship. His journey was a long and slow one around the Cape, with his ship docking in Liverpool in October 1940. Philby was imprisoned. The charge against him was for, "Activities prejudicial to the safety of the realm," a serious offense in a time of war.[32] He appealed his detention to the Home Office Advisory

Committee (HOAC). The HOAC requested Philby's file from the Foreign Office in order to judge the case. Minutes attached to the Foreign Office documents comment that, "On no account should they have the file." However, Stonehewer-Bird's telegrams were released as evidence.[33] Philby had his hearing before the HOAC on February 4, 1941. The decision was that he was a "harmless fanatic," and that he should be released. He regained his freedom on March 18th.[34] The war and Philby's own activities eclipsed his Palestine plan-- at least for a while.

Saudi Arabia Within a Regional Context, 1941

Ibn Saud was also experiencing an eclipse in 1941 as a result of the war. His problems were mainly economic and political. Revenues from the pilgrimage were the poorest since 1924, and Saudi Arabia was near bankruptcy. Britain added £500,000 to the previously promised £400,000 and, additionally, minted 10 million Riyals (£450,000) which were presented to Ibn Saud.[35] The King asked the American oil company, California Arabian Standard Oil, to provide additional advances on future oil royalties. The oil company advanced $7 million and recommended to President Roosevelt in May, that the American Government also advance funds to aid Saudi Arabia. America asked Great Britain to handle the loans to Saudi Arabia, using part of the $425 million America had just loaned her.[36] Thus America provided indirect aid. British and American aid enabled Ibn Saud to keep his country from bankruptcy, however, there was a year-end deficit of £1 million.

In the political arena of early 1941, Ibn Saud was one of the few Arabs with confidence in an eventual British victory in the war.

His own counsellors doubted Britain's ability to defeat Germany, especially after the H.M.S. Hood was lost and Britain's control of the sea was in jeopardy.[37] German-Italian forces were succeeding in their advance toward Egypt; Iraq was under the pro-Axis leader Rashid Ali; and Syria was under Vichy French control. Why should the Arabs listen to Ibn Saud and support a loser--especially one which allowed Zionists to continue entering Palestine? Ibn Saud advised the Arabs to have faith in Britain, she would keep her promises.[38]

Relations with Iraq and Transjordan were strained during the first months of 1941. Rashid Ali favored the Axis and the age-old border disputes regarding the Sammar tribes' territorial limits continued. Emir Abdullah tried to advise Ibn Saud on how to handle the Shereefian family which had plotted to overthrow his regime. The leader of the group was Sherif Abdul Hamid Ibn Ohn, a relative of Emir Abdullah.[39] Ibn Saud did not believe that Abdullah was implicated in the plot, only that he was too sympathetic with the guilty.[40] Relations with neighbors improved as the British proved Ibn Saud's forecast of victory to be correct. In May the British, with help from the Arab Legion in Transjordan, forced Rashid Ali out of Iraq (along with the Mufti of Jerusalem who had been there in exile) and reestablished pro-British Hashimite control.[41] When the British sank the Bismarck, Ibn Saud had his counsellors stands and applaud the news.

Dr. Weizmann As an Advocate

Having depicted Ibn Saud in perspective and the British attitude toward Philby, the next personality which must be addressed is that of Dr. Chaim Weizmann. While Ibn Saud counselled the Arabs to wait for the war to end before pursuing the Palestine question, the Jewish efforts to secure a homeland continued. For reasons unknown to this writer, Dr. Weizmann attempted in his autobiography to dis-associate himself from Philby's plan while in fact he was, next to Philby, its greatest advocate. Dr. Weizmann's account, Trial and Error (1949) bears little resemblance to the facts at hand. Philby, in Arabian Jubilee (1958), took issue with the Zionist leader's representation of the plan. He was very emotional in his appraisal of Dr. Weizmann and the other characters associated with the plan. Thus, the arguments of the plan's author are not sufficiently credible to stand alone. As Philby's plan and Dr. Weizmann's activities are further pursued, the latter's version will be comared with evidence derived from American State Department and British Foreign Office documents.

Dr. Weizmann visited Mr. Churchill at the British Admiralty Office on December 17, 1939, three days before the Jewish leader was to depart for the United States of America. They discussed the progress of the war, pending land legislation in Palestine, and Dr. Weizmann's post-war objective of a Jewish State with three to four million Jews. Churchill was "mindful" of the Jews and their problems, and agreed with the idea of building a Jewish State after the war.[42] Dr. Weizmann did not indicate in his autobiography whether or not he discussed Philby's plan with Mr. Churchill. However, it should be recalled that Brenden Bracken had informed Winston Churchill (a month and a half earlier) of Dr. Weizmann's enthusiasm for the plan.

The Jewish leader's account of his first trip to America noted that the country was "violently neutral" and that "one had to be careful of one's utterances."[43] He met with President Roosevelt and "tried to sound him out on the likelihood of American interest in a new departure in Palestine, away from the White Paper, when the War was over."[44] According to Dr. Weizmann the President kept the discussion "theoretical" but friendly. State Department documents record a meeting Dr. Weizmann had with Mr. Wallace Murray, Chief of the Division of Near Eastern Affairs, on February 6, 1940.[45] During this meeting the President of the World Zionist Organization expressed the view that the best solution to the Palestine question was the federation of Palestine and Trans-Jordan into one state with Jewish and Arab cantons generally along the lines of the 1937 partition scheme. The Negev, however, was to remain outside the cantonization plan for subsequent disposition. Dr. Weizmann indicated that after the War one million refugees would need to be settled in Palestine.[46] One fourth of the refugees would settle on the land and the remainder would become part of the urban population and develop industries. Mr. Murray asked why the Jews and Arabs were unable to reach an agreement. Dr. Weizmann's reply was that both the Jews and Arabs had to accept blame for the difficulties in Palestine. He also indicated that when Feisal died (1933) the Arabs were left without a single spokesman with whom he could negotiate. He then brought up Philby's plan, but with a major revision of the financial arrangements.

Referring to his meeting with Philby in 1939, Dr. Weizmann stated that he told Ibn Saud's friend that the only thing the Jews had to offer the Arabs was money. If Ibn Saud wanted a million

pounds - that was too little; if the King wanted fifteen or twenty
million pounds - that was beyond hope of realization by the Jews.
If the price were three to four million pounds, the Jews could raise
the sum.[47] This presentation is not consistent with what Dr. Weizmann
told the British. According to Brenden Bracken's memo to Churchill,
Dr. Weizmann indicated that the sum was twenty million pounds; and
that "Americans" were going to pay all of it. It would seem then
that Dr. Weizmann envisioned Jewish-Americans contributing up to
four million pounds and other Americans providing approximately sixteen
million pounds ($80,000,000). The Jewish leader ended his meeting
with Mr. Murray by stating that he felt Ibn Saud was an Arab with whom
he could deal. Consequently, he was anxious to hear from Philby
regarding Ibn Saud's response.[48] As was mentioned above, the only
response from Philby at this time was, "Progressing slowly." Dr.
Weizmann recorded in his autobiography that his first visit to America
was not a satisfactory one.[49] He was not discouraged though.

The Jewish leader made another three month visit to America in
the spring of 1941. His purpose was to tone down the Zionist's anti-
British propaganda rife in America.[50] The British government was
very concerned about the potential reactions in the Arab world to
the news that Americans were supporting the Zionist cause. The State
Department told the British Ambassador that it was difficult to deal
with the propaganda, for the American government could not inhibit
free speech.[51] State Department officials advised Dr. Weizmann's
representatives that they should consider the possible ramifications
if the Arabs turned against the British and forced them out of the
area. It was assumed by the State Department that the Jews did not

want to lose the protective screen between themselves and the Arabs in Palestine before a settlement was reached.[52] Dr. Weizmann worked to lessen the American Zionist's anxieties, but found it difficult to calm their emotional demands for a Jewish fighting force.[53] He continued his efforts to achieve the Zionist aspirations by maintaining contacts within both the American and British governments.

According to Dr. Weizmann, although Zionist aspirations were viewed sympathetically in the White House and at No. 10 Downing Street, the trouble he encountered always came from the Middle East experts in the State Department and Foreign Office.[54] His observation was valid. It is evident that, while aspects of the plan were considered positively, the bureaucrats reacted to the personalities involved, and their perceptions of their countries interests and therefore worked against it. This was the key factor in the demise of Philby's plan.

Very little is known of what transpired concerning Philby's plan during 1941. According to Philby, the British Prime Minister (Winston Churchill) was interested in the scheme and in November Dr. Weizmann was to see Anthony Eden (Secretary of State) on the subject.[55] The British Foreign Office file, pertaining to Philby in 1941, entitled, ... "Conversation at No. 10 Downing Street; his relation with Dr. Weizmann" is missing.[56] Philby's plan, although for the most part dormant in 1941, resurfaced at No. 10 Downing Street within a year of its author's release from confinement.

Dr. Weizmann's account indicates that on March 11 he was en-route to the airport for his departure to America, and stopped by No. 10 Downing Street to say good-bye to Churchill's private

secretary, Mr. John Martin. As Weizmann was about to leave, Mr.
Martin decided to take the Jewish leader to see Mr. Churchill. The
Prime Minister wished him luck on his trip and then, to the complete
surprise of Dr. Weizmann, stated:

> "I want you to know that I have a plan, which
> of course can only be carried into effect when
> the war is over. I would like to see Ibn Saud
> made Lord of the Middle East - the boss of
> the bosses - provided he settles with you. It
> will be up to you to get the best possible
> conditions. Of course we shall help you. Keep
> this confidential, but you might talk it over
> with Roosevelt when you get to America. There's
> nothing he and I cannot do if we set our minds
> on it."

The "monologue" rendered by Churchill "dazed" Dr. Weizmann to the
extent that there was no discussion of the Prime Minister's plan and
the Jewish leader departed.[57] Dr. Weizmann then recalled an
incomprehensible "offer" he had received a few months before from
Ibn Saud's confidant - St. John Philby. According to Dr. Weizmann,
Philby said that Churchill and Roosevelt "should tell Ibn Saud that
they wished to see your program through" and that they would "support
his overlordship of the Arab countries and raise a loan for him to
enable him to develop his territories."[58] This representation, if
believed, would absolve Dr. Weizmann from any responsibility for
the furtherance of Philby's plan or its failure. Churchill and Philby
would be viewed as the advocates and not Dr. Weizmann.

When Dr. Weizmann left No. 10 Downing Street he wrote a memorandum
on his meeting with Churchill. He gave it to an aide for safekeeping.
In the event that his plane crashed the Jewish leadership would
receive this very important memo. The biographers of Dr. Weizmann
state that he went to No. 10 Downing Street to visit Brenden Bracken,

not Mr. Martin. It was Bracken who first represented Dr. Weizmann's interest in the plan back in 1939. The statement attributed to Mr. Churchill is basically the same as that given above, but it does not refer to Ibn Saud as "Boss of Bosses" or "Lord of the Middle East" - only "Lord of the Arab countries."[59] The latter version is probably the correct one. Mr. Churchill was too familiar with the "Middle East" to make such a statement.

Philby's rebuttal of Dr. Weizmann's account took issue with latter's incorrect representation of his departure date and that they had discussed his plan in October 1939 as well as in 1942. The significance of this is that Philby met with Dr. Weizmann at lunch on March 9th and on March 17th.[60] Philby did not publish what the two discussed at those lunches. It is unlikely, however, that the Jewish leader would not have discussed his meeting with Mr. Churchill. The New York Times recorded Dr. Weizmann's arrival in the United States, via a Pan American flight, on April 15, 1942.[61]

Upon arriving in America, Dr. Weizmann paid a brief visit to President Roosevelt, but did not discuss "Churchill's plan."[62] His visit was not as a Jewish leader but as a scientist who was to develop synthetic rubber for the war effort. In May he took some time away from his scientific efforts and participated in an American Zionist's conference at the Biltmore Hotel in New York City. The conference adopted a resolution which embodied the Zionist's objectives. The "Biltmore Program" of May 11, 1942 expressed: a readiness for full cooperation with Palestine's Arab neighbors; rejection of the 1939 White Paper as immoral and illegal; a demand for a Jewish military force; a desire to have the Jewish Agency control immigration and land development; and finally, the establishment of a Jewish Commonwealth.[63] Dr. Weizmann spoke effectively at the conference and thereafter supported the resolution.[64] The program was ineffectively opposed by moderate Zionists and the anti-Zionist Rabbis.[65] With a firm resolution the American-Jewish community launched a major lobbying effort to gather support for their cause.[66]

Dr. Weizmann approached Summer Welles (Under Secretary of State) with "secret information" on December 4, 1942. He informed Mr. Welles that Mr. Churchill wanted to make Ibn Saud the "boss of bosses" in the Arab World (not Middle East) if the King was willing to work out a sane solution of the Palestine question with Dr. Weizmann. Mr. Churchill was also reported to have stated that President Roosevelt was in agreement with the plan. This is interesting in that Dr. Weizmann's earlier account of Mr. Churchill's statement to him failed to mention President Roosevelt's knowledge and support of the plan. Mr. Welles noted that he had never heard the President express such an opinion. Dr. Weizmann was anxious to establish a contact with the State Department to discuss the future of Palestine. Mr. Welles sent a memo on the meeting to Mr. Wallace Murray (Advisor on Political Relations) for his comment.[67]

Mr. Murray's reply of December 17, 1942, focused on three points. The first addressed the fact that Ibn Saud was, due to his own efforts, already the master of the heart of the Arab world, and probably would not relish the idea of being made "boss of the bosses" by the British. There was little likelihood that he would consider trying to control even the "fertile crescent" of Iraq, Syria, Lebanon and Palestine; let alone all of the "Arab World" (which would include North Africa). Conceivably he might consider an extension to include Transjordan. Ibn Saud was considered an unsurpassed Bedouin King, but not qualified to govern the more settled and developed town Arabs.

The second point related to the condition that Ibn Saud agree to Dr. Weizmann's "sane" solution. Ibn Saud, as the temporal leader of the Wahhabis, would not likely, "under the present circumstances" acquiesce to the Zionists "in their present state of mind." The "circumstances" Mr. Murray referred to were that the British had reversed the Axis tide and seemed to be maintaining their position on the 1939 White Paper. Why then should the Arabs give up any territory to the Zionists? The Zionist "Biltmore Program" was a maximalist position from which the Arabs could see no definite gain. Mr. Murry thought that talks might be undertaken if Dr. Weizmann could provide Ibn Saud assurances which renounced political Zionism and the idea of Jewish control over any large section of Arabs resulting from immigration. Furthermore, the Arab leaders from Iraq, Syria and Egypt would have to be involved unless Ibn Saud was to be imposed on the Arab world. The modus vivendi Mr. Murray preferred was that recommended by Dr. Magnes of the Hebrew University in Jerusalem: a bi-national state with an Arab majority.

Mr. Murray's final point was that the State Department had very reliable information, from competent observers (unnamed) in Saudi Arabia, indicating that Ibn Saud wanted to lessen his dependency on Great Britain (which controlled all of the territories around Saudi Arabia) and establish a closer relationship with America. America's

interests in Arabia were growing. Oil concessions and projected
air route requirements for American civilian aviation were already
significant subjects of discussion within the State Department.
Mr. Murray concluded his memo with the observation that any effort to
facilitate an understanding between the Zionists and Arab leaders
should be a joint American-British one.[68]

Philby would have certainly agreed with Mr. Murray's last
observation, since that is what he proposed three years earlier.
However, Dr. Weizmann had not presented Philby's plan, in its entirety,
to Mr. Murray in their February 1940 meeting. In that meeting the
Jewish leader focused only on the monetary aspect of Philby's plan
with no mention of British or American government guarantees. It
can only be surmised that Dr. Weizmann, at that time, considered
America's neutrality and aversion toward involvement and therefore
sought only that form of contribution which was palatable, money.
By the end of 1942 America's perspective of the Middle East had
changed, and the United States was beginning to become more involved
in the region.

Arab and Zionist Attitudes

At this time the State Department and the Joint Chiefs of Staff
were becoming concerned that American troops might be needed to help
the British in the Near East since Rommel was pushing hard toward El
Alamein. If American troops were to go they did not want the Arabs
to be anti-American. President Roosevelt decided to send a military/
ecnomic mission into the region to assess the situation and to
reinforce America's political contacts. The head of the mission was
Lieutenant Colonel (Ltc.) Harold B. Hoskins. He was born in Beirut

of American missionary parents and spoke Arabic, French, German and Spanish. During the inter-war period he had been a cotton goods businessman in southern Europe and the Near East. He returned to service and worked for the State Department as Middle East specialist, while maintaining his position as Vice-President of the Board of Trustees of the American University of Beirut. After a period of polite negotiations with the British to obtain their agreement, Ltc. Hoskins departed in November, 1942 on what would be a three and a half month trip.[69]

On January 23, 1943 Ltc. Hoskins sent Under Secretary Welles an interim report which expressed great concern about the high probability of renewed fighting between the Arabs and Jews. He expected the fighting to errrupt within a few months unless positive steps were taken. His assessment was based on the hardening attitudes on both sides. The Zionist officials of the Jewish Agency were outspoken in their determination for a Jewish State, despite the opposition of the Arabs. The Zionists were confident that they had the support of public opinion in Great Britain and the United States; and they believed their increase in population and arms would enable them militarily to defeat the Palestinian Arabs. The Arabs feared that the Great Powers were going to hand over Palestine to the Jews. Nazi propaganda (in Arabic) constantly played on the Arab fears and suspicions. Ltc. Hoskins recommended that the United States and Britain make a joint settlement which would rule out in advance any allied military support for either Arab or Zionist extreme positions. Also, the American public should be informed of both sides of the situation by inviting Emir Abdullah and several Arab moderates from Palestine,

Syria, Lebanon, and Trans-Jordan, as well as Jewish moderates such
as Dr. J. L. Magnes, to isit the United States. In effect he
proposed that America offer its "good offices" to facilitate a
moderate solution.[70]

Under Secretary Welles responded to Ltc. Hoskins on January 28,
stating that the latter's report was being given careful thought.
"Our present feeling is that it would be inadvisable to bring groups
of Arabs and Jews to this country for a discussion of the Palestine
problem. However; the suggestion has been made that Ibn Saud be
asked to designate one of his three eldest sons to come here for a
visit." It was realized that the King might not consider it advisable
to make the trip himself.[71] Evidently Dr. Weizmann's discussions with
Mr. Welles had their affect.

Dr. Weizmann and his Political Advisor, Mr. Moshe Shertok, met
with Mr. Murray on 3 March 1943 to discuss the future of Palestine.[72]
As a preface to the meeting, Dr. Weizmann tried to deprecate the
unfavorable remarks of certain Army officers who had spent too little
time in Palestine to gain a true understanding of the situation, a
veiled reference to Ltc. Hoskins who had just returned to Washington
in February. Mr. Shertok spoke of the many contributions the Jews
had already made in Palestine. He then suggested that, if large
numbers of Jews were allowed to settle there, they could make use of
the enormous potential for development. The result would be
economically advantageous to both the United States and Britain. The
Arabs were an underdeveloped people who would benefit from the
Jewish enterprises in Palestine and the neighborning states.
Palestine, according to Mr. Shertok, was "an Arab country ro longer."

When Mr. Murray doubted that the Arabs would agree with that statement, Mr. Shertok acknowledged that there would be resistance but that it could be overcome if large numbers of Jews were admitted to Palestine as quickly as possible.

The discussion then turned to how the Jews envisioned their future relationship with the Arabs. Mr. Shertok stated that Ibn Saud was the most important Arab alive, one who might serve as the head of a Pan-Arab Union, but not as a ruler of an Arab empire. Obviously the Zionists would not want a unified Arab power surrounding Palestine. Mr. Shertok thought that a meeting between Dr. Weizmann or a Jewish delegation and Ibn Saud was not possible. But he did believe that a British or American representative could discuss matters with Ibn Saud without it being known to others. It was assumed that the King's reply would be negative, but a perceptive interviewer could judge the degree of his negative reaction and interpret its true meaning. When Mr. Murray addressed the negative attitude of Ibn Saud's letter to the President in 1938 (Appendix E) Mr. Weizmann remarked that Ibn Saud wrote it because "no Arab could afford to speak less loudly than the other."[73] They then resummed their discussion on the future of Palestine.

Dr. Weizmann declared that "Palestine will never again be an Arab country."[74] He stated that the United States had a moral responsibility toward Palestine. The Jews had spent money on Palestine and would bring moral pressure to bear on the government in order to create a Jewish Palestine. Those Jews who feared expulsion from America if a Jewish State was created were considered foolish and few in number. Thus the Zionist's aspirations were obvious. They envisioned a Jewish State as an economic center of the region and Ibn Saud as the Arab leader of the neighboring states.

Ibn Saud indeed saw himself as the leader of the Arabs, but he was also the leader of the Moslims. Alexander C. Kirk, the American Minister to Egypt and Saudi Arabia, visited Ibn Saud in early April to discuss lend-lease matters, but as he was about to depart the King delayed him for a confidential meeting concerning Palestine and Syria. He said that Palestine was of more concern to him than to any other Arab leader - because Jews had been hostile to Arabs from the time of Prophet Mohammed, and he (Ibn Saud) as the leading Arab and Moslem had a special interest in Palestine. The Jews because of their wealth were encroaching on Arabs. If this continued there would be conflict which would disrupt the Allied war effort. He said that other Arabs had asked him to make public declarations on the Palestine issue, but he refrained for two reasons: 1) He had previously written the President and received his "neutral" reply (1938); 2) He did not want to create a problem for the United States and divert its attention from the war. If he wrote to the President and the reply was favorable to only one side Jewish or Arab, the other would cause trouble.

Ibn Saud demonstrated an acute sense of statesmanship in this observation. In effect, he primed President Roosevelt for a forthcoming letter. He then told Kirk that if it were not for these conditions he would be obligated to act. He was additionally concerned that during his silence America might respond favorably to one of the other Arab leaders' proposals and thereby cause him to be perceived as an uninterested bystander. Ibn Saud asked that the President indicate whether or not he agreed with his policy of silence. If so, the

King wanted an assurance that he would be informed in advance of any steps America took with other Arabs, so he could consider adjusting his policy. If not, the King had a plan of action in mind.[75] He did not say what his plan was, but it subsequently became evident that he considered launching a strong public information program to counter the near monopoly enjoyed by the Zionists.[76]

The King also stressed that he had no territorial ambitions and only wanted Palestine and Syria to be independent "alongside Saudi Arabia and Iraq in a balanced comity of Arab states."[77] He was very concerned that the Pan-Arab proposals then circulating were designed to create a Hashimite bloc. In view of the traditional hositility between the Hashimites and the House of Saud, the King was hopeful that the Allies would not allow such a serious threat to Saudi Arabia to develop. He concluded his conversation with Mr. Kirk by stressing the confidentiality of his statements and asked that they be revealed to no one, not even the British. Mr. Kirk conveyed the King's message to the President and added a personal observation:

> "...it is difficult if not impossible without incurring the criticisms of hyperbole or even emotionalisms, adequately to reflect the sincerity of the King and the profound conviction in the virtue of his own judgment. He is simple, honest and decisive and these qualities transcend the limited formula of his special experience. He believes that we are his friends and to him friendship bespeaks complete confidence. Compromise is inadmissable. He truly feels that his problems are ours and ours are his and in giving this message for the President, he confirmed throughout an absolute faith is the justice of the democracies and a conviction that the order which is to follow their victory will justify that faith."[78]

Thus the King, through confidential channels, conveyed his personal

position on Palestine. On April 30, 1943, King Abdul Aziz Ibn
Saud dispatched a formal letter to President Roosevelt expressing
his concern about Palestine and Zionist activities. But before the
King's letter arrived, President Roosevelt received two reports from
his personal representatives to the Middle East.

Brigadier General (BG) Patrick J. Hurley sent a report from
Cairo to the President on May 5, 1943.[79] He stated that, as he
saw it, the Zionist organization was committed to: 1) a Jewish State
which embraced Palestine and probably Transjordan, 2) eventual
transfer of the Arab population to Iraq, 3) Jewish economic leadership
for the whole Middle East. The General recounted a discussion with
Mr. Ben-Gurion, the Zionist leader in Palestine, whose argument was
that "the Government of the United States is committed and obligated,
repeat obligated, to establish a Jewish Political State in Palestine."[80]
The "obligation" was derived from Scriptural promises, historical
logic, and the investment of Jewish-American capital. Not all Jews
shared the Zionist position but their true position was hard to
assess because the Jewish Agency controlled their livelihood. On the
Arab side BG Hurley reported little or no anti-Jewish sentiment but
strong opposition to a Jewish State. Some of the hostility was
toward the "chosen people" concept which was regarded as kindred to
Nazi doctrine. Auni Bey Abdul Hadi, leader of the Arab Moslem
majority in Palestine, indicated that the United States was perceived
as the main supporter of the Zionists, and was forcing the British
to acquiesce in the establishment of a Jewish State.[81] This was
considered as a British attempt to bolster their position with the
Arabs. BG Hurley reported that the Arab proposal which received

majority support in the region was that of Nuri Pasha es-Said,
Prime Minister of Iraq. The Iraqi plan would establish an Arab
Federation "embracing Palestine, Transjordan, the Lebanon, Syria,
Iraq and such other Arab states as might desire." The Jews and
Christians would have autonomous rights in those districts where they
constituted a majority.[82]

Cordell Hull, Secretary of State, submitted Ltd. Hoskins' report
of his three and one half month survey of the Near East to President
Roosevelt on May 7th; indicating that the report summary (Appendix H)
warranted careful reading.[83] Ltc. Hoskins depicted in Part I of
his report: the growing tension between the Arabs and Jews; the
potential for problems in North Africa for American troops; the need
to inform the American people of the Arab view; and the assessment
that only military force could impose a Zionist State on the Arabs.
Part II noted the disunity in America with increasing anti-Semitism
due to an inappropriate mixing of the two separate issues of humanitarian support for the persecuted Jews in Europe, and the Zionist's
aspirations. Part III suggested that the Arabs would continue
supporting the Allies if the United States assured them that no
final decisions regarding Palestine would be made until after the
war and then only after full consultation with both Arabs and Jews.
Part IV outlined a post-war solution which would: not transfer Arabs
or Jews into new territories; form a binational state (with the Jews
allowed to immigrate until parity was reached) within a Levant
Federation (Lebanon, Syria, Palestine and Transjordan); place the
Holy Places under United Nations control; and provide territory for
a Jewish States in the virtually uninhabited (but cultivable) northern

Cirenaica in Liby   The President read the report and, as it will be
seen, implemented some of its recommendations.

The State Department received Ibn Saud's letter of April 30th
on May 25th (Appendix J). In it the King expressed his alarm that
while the Allies were engaged in a War to defend freedom and liberty,
the Zionists were misleading the American public in order to gain
support for the eviction of Arabs and the installation of Jews in
Palestine. He referred to, his November 1938 letter in which he had
provided an historical argument against the Jewish claim. The King
assumed that the President since he had not commented on the facts
presented, understood the Arab position and would so inform the American
public. As for the Jewish refugee problem, the King suggested that
it would be solved if each of the Allied countries accepted just
ten percent of the number that Palestine had. His specific request
was that "you should hlep to stop the flow of migration by finding
a place for the Jews to live in other than Palestine, and by preventing completely the sale of lands to them." The King was sure that
the President and the American people were fighting "to ensure to
every people its freedom and to grant it its rights. For if--God
forbid!--Jews were to be granted their desire, Palestine would forever remain a hotbed of troubles and disturbances as in the past."[84]
Ibn Saud's letter must have arrived as a message from President
Roosevelt was being dispatched by Cordell Hull on May 26th.

It is obvious that President Roosevelt considered Ibn Saud's
earlier confidential message as well as the reports from BG Hurley
and Ltc. Hoskins when he drafted his response (Appendix K). The
King had asked if he should maintain his policy of silence on the

Arab issues. The President agreed that "continued silence with
respect to such matters would prove most helpful..." But he also
told the King that it would be highly desirable if the Arabs and Jews
could reach an agreement on Palestine before the War was over. He
provided the King the assurance that he asked for, and that Ltc.
Hoskins recommended, by stating "that no decision altering the basic
situation in Palestine should be reached without full consultation
with both Arabs and Jews."[85] After the President received Ibn Saud's
letter he sent another message on June 19th (Appendix L), reiterating
the one he had just sent. He added that he "noted carefully" the
King's letter of November 1938 as well as the recent oral message relayed by Kirk and his letter of April 30th. The President did not
restate his desire that Ibn Saud remain silent on Arab issues. The
King had already had an interview in Riyadh with Life Editor Noel
Busch on March 21st. The President's message of May 26th asking the
King to maintain silence was not given to Amir Faisal, Minister of
Foreign Affairs, until June 6th.[86]

The King's interview appeared in the May 31, 1943 issue of Life
(Appendix M). He expressed his opinion on the Palestine problem in
basically the same way he had to President Roosevelt one month earlier,
but more briefly. He knew of nothing that justified Jewish claims. Their
claims created problems between the Moslems and the Allies and served
no good. Europe and America were larger, more fertile, and more
suited to the Jewish interests than Palestine. He believed that the
native Jews in Palestine would be safeguarded if they caused no
trouble and if they guaranteed, with Allied endorsements, that they
would buy no more Arab property.[87]

If there ever was a chance for Philby's plan to be the bridge between the Jews and Ibn Saud, the King, in that interview burned it. Why? If we assume Ibn Saud considered Philby's proposal in January 1940, how might he have viewed it in May of 1943? It had been over three years since Philby told the King that the British and American heads of state were going to make their offers. During that time the only things that the King knew for sure was that Philby had been arrested by the British; that the British still professed adherence to the 1939 White Paper and continued their financial aid to him; that American interests in oil were growing and that his royalties should increase after the War; that the Zionists were growing in strength; that other Arab leaders were proposing solutions which were detrimental to his vital interests; and lastly, his continued silence was detrimental to his standing in the Moslem world. Ibn Saud's statements in Life were obviously for public consumption in America and in the Muslim world. They seemed to reflect his sincere personal convictions. His statement gained him a great deal of moral and political prestige throughout the Moslem world.[88] There certainly was no longer any chance that he might support Philby's plan.

The King's statements did not however stop Dr. Weizmann or Philby from continuing their efforts to implement the latter's plan. Their continued efforts reveal Philby's naive and myopic view of the political factors involved; and Dr. Weizmann's manipulative methods in the pursuit of his objectives.

Philby met with Gladwyn Jebb, head of the British Foreign Office, post-war planning section, at lunch on June 8, 1943, and presented his scheme.[89] Philby proposed that the British and French withdraw

from the region and give the Jews dominion status in Palestine up
to the Jordan. Ibn Saud could then establish an Arab State (blood-
lessly) from Aleppo to Oman. The Jews would then finance a gradual
evacuation of all the Arabs from Palestine to Ibn Saud's territory.
Mr. Jebb expressed doubt about the Shi'a inhabitants of Iraq or the
Imam of Yemen accepting such a move; to which Philby stated that
Ibn Saud could manage it with very little fighting. In his memo, Mr.
Jebb evaluated Philby's scheme as "chimerical, but I wonder
if there are a lot of points in it which we might conceivably explore
further?" The idea of using money to obtain British base_ in a Jewish
country and to establish Ibn Saud as an ally was attractive. The four
other officials who minuted Mr. Jebb's memo disagreed. They were not
willing to buy Palestine for the Jews by withdrawing from everywhere
else, nor did they believe British interests would be protected by
the Zionists. "We should find a purely Jewish State far more national-
istic and far less ready to give us what we want than any Arab State."[90]

Dr. Weizmann, accompanied by Sumner Welles, met with President
Roosevelt on June 11, 1943. According to Dr. Weizmann's memo to the
British Foreign Office, the President began the discussion by stating
that he had persuaded Mr. Churchill to agree to calling together a
meeting of the Jews and Arabs and to attending that meeting with him.[91]
Dr. Weizmann remarked that such a meeting would end as the 1939 St.
James Conference in London had unless the Arabs were told beforehand
that the Democracies meant to affirm Jewish rights to Palestine. He
believed that action was required before the war was over. The
President decided to send Ltc. Hoskins, rather than Philby, to Ibn
Saud to determine whether or not the King would enter into discussions

with Dr. Weizmann or any other Jewish Agency representative.[92] In
accordance with the President's instructions, Mr. Churchill's concur-
rence was obtained before Ltc. Hoskins was sent on his mission.[93]

Ltc. Hoskins went to Saudi Arabia in August, and for eight days
had daily conversations (in Arabic and often alone) with the King.
He first asked the King whether or not he would meet with Dr. Weizmann
to discuss the Palestine problem. Ibn Saud declined to answer until
he considered the matter. After a few days Ltc. Hoskins presented an
alternative question: would the King, if he would not meet Dr.
Weizmann, appoint a representative to meet outside the country with
Dr. Weizmann or his representative? At the end of the week Ibn Saud
refused both propositions. The refusal was based on religious and
patriotic principles. The King could not speak for the people of
Palestine without consultation, much less "deliver" Palestine to
the Jews. Ibn Saud said he hated Dr. Weizmann because of an attempted
bribe in 1940. Philby had conveyed the Zionist's bribe offer of
£20 million sterling, which was to be guaranteed by President Roosevelt
Ltc. Hoskins report indicated that the King's attitudes toward the
Jewish question in Palestine had not changed from that which he
expressed in his letters of November 1938 and April 1943, and his Life
interview. He concluded that Dr. Weizmann and Philby misinterpreted
the King's silence regarding the plan. He did not believe Ibn Saud
would ever help the Zionists in Palestine.[94]

On September 27th Ltc. Hoskins briefed President Roosevelt on
his visit with Ibn Saud. The President was surprised and irritated
that his name was falsely given as guarantor of payment for a bribe.

He said that the only suggestion he ever made, that even bordered
the subject, was in a talk with Dr. Steven Wise, an American Zionist
leader, several years earlier, in which he had suggested that if
the Jews wished more land in Palestine they might think of buying
arable land outside of Palestine and financially assist the Palestinian
Arabs to move there. Ltc. Hoskins emphasized "that the establishment
of a Jewish State in Palestine [could] only be imposed by force and
[could] only be maintained by force." The President stated that his
own thinking on a solution was leaning toward a Holy Land trusteeship
with Jews, Christians, and Moslems responsible for it. Ltc. Hoskins
believed such a plan might be agreed to by the Arabs if they were
guaranteed that Palestine would never become a Jewish State.[95] The
President sent Ltc. Hoskins to London to brief Mr. Churchill and
the British Foreign Office on his mission to Saudi Arabia and to
inform Dr. Weizmann of Ibn Saud's position regarding Palestine.[96]

The British Foreign Office was pleased to note that the Roosevelt
Administration: "1) now understand and wish to avoid the danger of
encouraging the Zionists, and 2) are beginning to understand that it
is a Moslem as well as an Arab issue..."[97] It is not known by this
writer whether or not Ltc. Hoskins ever briefed Mr. Churchill.

While in London, Ltc. Hoskins met with Dr. Weizmann and
told him that Ibn Saud referred to him "in the angriest and most
contemptuous manner" because of his attempt to bribe the King. Also,
it was Ltc. Hoskins contention that the King would never permit
Philby "to cross the frontiers of his Kingdom."[98] Dr. Weizmann arranged
to have Philby visit Ltc. Hoskins on November 15, 1943. Philby wrote
a lengthy memorandum on this meeting and gave it to Dr. Weizmann.

What the latter did with the memorandum will be addressed below.
According to Dr. Weizmann's autobiography "nothing came of the plan"
after Ltc. Hoskins returned from seeing Ibn Saud.[99] That is a fact,
as an end result, but it does not reflect his efforts to revive the
plan.

Final Efforts of Dr. Weizmann and Philby

It seems that Dr. Weizmann had a tendency, when communicating
with someone, to adjust his arrangement of facts according to his
objectives at the time. On August 31st Dr. Weizmann visited Colonel
Oliver Stanley, British Colonial Secretary, to check on various
matters of interest to him regarding Palestine. When he referred to
Ibn Saud's role he said that the Prime Minister (Churchill) had
originated the idea of making Ibn Saud the leader among Arab rulers
in return for a scheme for Palestine acceptable to the Jews. After-
wards, he met Philby who told him that £20,000,000 promised to Ibn
Saud would result in a satisfactory solution.[100] One can surmise,
from the above, that either Weizmann decided that it would be
beneficial to his cause to have a British subject believe that his
Prime Minister originated the plan, or Stanley misunderstood. To
infer that the former is probably the case is made easier when one
recalls a similar approach used when Dr. Weizmann first spoke to
Sumner Welles and said that President Roosevelt favored the plan, and
when one looks at what Dr. Weizmann did in conjunction with Philby's
monograph.

On December 13, 1943 Dr. Weizmann sent a letter to Mr. Welles
asking him to pursue Philby's scheme with the President (Appendix N).

It is evident in paragraph 2 that he first discussed the plan with Philby in 1939, not 1942 as he indicates in Trial and Error. Also in paragraph 2 he presents a partial truth when he states that the Jews would finance the re-settlement of Arabs in the form of "goods." Mr. Namier's memo (Appendix G) reveals that a major form of "goods" was to be in arms, as well as land development. It is easily understand-able why such an omission occurred.[101] In the first sentence of paragraph 5 he disclaims the assertion of a United States guarantee of money, but in the last sentence he contradicts himself by suggesting that Philby's scheme "be offered to Ibn Saud on behalf of the President and Mr. Churchill." Dr. Weizmann then referred Mr. Welles to Mr. Philby's comments which were enclosed. Philby's original note is at Appendix O. It has been annotated to reflect those portions not included in Dr. Weizmann's "extracts" and those portions that were revised. It can not be determined precisely who made the revisions, but it is obvious that the original note would not have enhanced Dr. Weizmann's position. The exclusion of Philby's tactless and barbed comments directed at the British and American Governments is understandable. However, the editing of Philby's note also eliminated the fact that Philby believed that the two governments had been fully aware of his plan since 1939. Also eliminated was the fact that Philby could not fathom why Hoskins was not aware of his plan. Philby was so naive and myopic toward his plan that he could not conceive of anyone else manipulating him or his plan for their own purposes. Philby's personal file copy did not indicate that subsequent revisions or deletions were made.[102] Mr. Welles' response to this correspondence is unknown. President Roosevelt did subsequently arrange a personal meeting with Ibn Saud, which will be discussed below.

Dr. Weizmann sent a copy of his letter to Mr. Welles to Sir George Gater, Colonial Office Permanent Under-Secretary, on December 20, 1943. It was then sent to the Foreign Office. The minutes attached to the letter and its "extract" enclosure clearly reveal the official reactions. "It is evidence of Philby's pigheadedness...", "Anyone who thinks Ibn Saud will look at this hair-brained scheme after what he has said about it, must be quite cracked. This [correspondence] does Mr. Weizmann no credit." Sir Maurice Peterson, Under Secretary of State for Foreign Affairs sent a copy of the letter to Sir Ronald Campbell, British Minister in the United States, on January 25, 1944. He stated that "Weizmann is still trying to press Philby's fantastic plan for Palestine, involving the buying of Ibn Saud's consent...," furthermore it "takes no account at all of British interests in the Arab countries, which are all to be sacrificed for the sake of the Zionists..." His concluding opinion was that nothing but harm would come from further efforts to press the plan, and he hoped Sir Ronald would express that view if he heard the subject raised.[103] The subject, minus Ibn Saud's role, was raised again, but not in America.

In Trial and Error, Dr. Weizmann records the fact that he continued to press his case, in 1943 and 1944, with the British Laborites. But when he addressed the April 1944 report of the Labor Party National Executive Committee he disavowed the measures they recommended in support of a Jewish National Home. The report read in part:

> "Let the Arabs be encouraged to move out as
> the Jews move in. Let them be compensated
> handsomely for their land, and their settle-
> ment elsewhere be carefully organized and
> generously financed."

Dr. Weizmann wrote that he and his Labor Zionist friends were greatly

concerned about the proposal. "We had never contemplated the removal

of the Arabs...," the Laborites went far beyond his intentions.[104]

It is obvious that, in advocating Philby's plan to the British and

American Governments, Dr. Weizmann did envision the transfer of Arabs

outside of Palestine to facilitate the development of a Jewish entity.

We also know that the Zionists agreed to finance the transfer, either

in land development or goods. The Labor Party recommendation did

have two drawbacks if one looks at it negatively. It only "encouraged"

the Arabs to move out, and it also called for generously financed re-

settlement after the Arabs were compensated handsomely. The words

"handsomely" and "generously" would naturally cause an "impoverished"

Jewry concern if the Labor Party's proposal were accepted as official

policy. The proposal was effectively opposed by both Jews and Arabs.[105]

Thus the last semblance of Philby's plan came to an end.

In his book, Arabian Jubilee (1953), Philby lamented the demise

of his plan, attributing its failure to the impact of Ltc. Hoskin's

report on President Roosevelt and Mr. Churchill.[106] His criticism

of the two heads of state typifies his extreme manner:

> "The full blame for the bloodshed and misery
> that preceded the final settlement rests
> fairly and squarely on the shoulders of the
> two men who could have solved the problem
> peacefully, if they had set their minds to
> it."

He believed that all they had to do was try it. Philby had told Ibn

Saud that the "plan" was to be proposed by the highest authorities in the world, and he need not commit himself until they approached him. Philby was bitter that the two heads of state did not "condescend to seek elucidation of its (the plans) details and prospects from its author "because of pride and prejudice. And because they were not willing to try the unorthodox, or submit the Palestine question to the International Court, they played "the orthodox political game of trying to get as much as possible for the Jews after the war without committing themselves to any quid pro quo for the Arabs." Philby did not consider the fact that Dr. Weizmann was the communicator of his "plan" to both President Roosevelt and Mr. Churchill.

Ibn Saud and F. D. Roosevelt

Although Philby wrote his severely critical remarks about President Roosevelt in 1953, he failed to address the President's meeting with Ibn Saud in 1945. In November 1944 Ibn Saud sent word to President Roosevelt that he would like to see him.[107] As President Roosevelt was preparing to depart the Yalta Conference Stalin asked him if he were going to make any concessions to Ibn Saud. The President replied that he intended to review the entire Palestine question with the King. Their rendezvous was arranged to be aboard the U.S.S. Murphy, in the Great Bitter Lake in the Suez Canal, on February 14, 1945.

At one of the King's desert encampments enroute to Jedda (where he was to secretly board an American destroyer) Ibn Saud received an unexpected visitor, David Van Der Meulen, the Minister from the Netherlands. Van Der Meulen was not aware of the King's forthcoming meeting and was enroute to meet the King in Riyadh. He was fluent in Arabic and attended the King's afternoon meeting of his Court

(tribal leaders and Ulema) and noted the King's attitude toward

the Yahud - the Jews.

> "He reminded his listeners of their (the Jews)
> history, full as it was of rebellion against
> Allah. He pointed to the role they had play-
> ed in world history where they had been harmful
> to nearly every nation in whose midst they had
> lived. The Yahud are our arch-enemies...."

But the King did not advocate a Hitlerite policy. In the world the

King envisioned...

> "Even the Yahudis would be treated like guests
> in Arab countries but on one condition: that
> they should behave like guests. Not like the
> Zionists in Palestine who were driving a small,
> weak Arab people away from the soil of their
> fathers and who dared to refer to that land as
> the land of THEIR fathers, may they be cursed![108]

The King proceeded to quote from the Koran those texts which recounted

the bitterness of Muhammed's conflict with the Jews in Medina. As

he recited the Koran Ibn Saud was not only the King, he was the Imam.[109]

The next day Ibn Saud, the King and Imam, departed Saudi Arabia to

meet President Roosevelt.

The two leaders met on the top deck of the U.S.S. Murphy, and

exchanged the appropriate greetings. They then proceeded to a private

conference room. According to Colonel William A. Eddy, the interpretor,

the only attendees during the political discussion were the President,

Ibn Saud, Yusuf Yassin (the King's political secretary) and himself.

The meeting lasted "at least five very intense hours."[110] President

Roosevelt told Ibn Saud that he had committed himself to finding a

solution for the Jewish victims of the Nazi horror, and asked if the

King had any suggestions. Ibn Saud replied: "Given them and their

decendents the choicest lands and homes of the Germans who had oppressed them."[111] The President related that the Jews did not want to stay in Germany, but wanted to settle in Palestine. He was counting on Arab hospitality and the King's help to solve the problem of Zionism. Ibn Saud's reply was that one should, "Make the enemy and oppressor pay; that is how we Arabs wage war. Amends should be made by the criminal, not by the innocent bystander."[112] The King's position on the refugees was that they should be distributed among the Allies according to each countries ability to support them. Palestine had already been assigned more than its quota. Colonel Eddy noted that at no time did Ibn Saud even hint at economic of financial aid for Saudi Arabia. The King, as an Arab guest, initiated no topics. The only thing he asked of the President was his friendship and support for Saudi Arabia's continued independence. If Philby's plan was to be discussed, it would have had to be raised by the President. Colonel Eddy's account made no mention of anything resembling Philby's plan.

The only other evidence available which provides any basis for assessing the President's meeting with Ibn Saud is in his subsequent conversation with his acting Secretary of State, Edward R. Stettinius, Jr. According to Mr. Stettinius, the President:

> "told me that he must have a conference with congressional leaders and re-examine our entire policy on Palestine. He was now convinced, he added, that if nature took its course there would be bloodshed between the Arabs and Jews. Some formula, not yet discovered, would have to be evolved to prevent this warfare, he concluded."[113]

It is evident that Philby's plan was not considered to be a possible solution. Either the President discounted it beforehand and did not broach it or, if it was discussed it was not accepted.

Dr. Weizmann's resubmission of Philby's plan to President Roosevelt probably provided the President a basis for thinking that a negotiated settlement was still possible. If in 1943 there were no chance that the Arabs would allow further immigration, the President would have then had to reconsider his policies toward Palestine. But it is obvious that he still thought there was a possiblity that Ibn Saud would help him with his Zionist problem. Once President Roosevelt met Ibn Saud he had to face the irrebutable facts. After learning what the true Arab position was first hand, he planned to re-examine his Palestine policy. But as we know, he died shortly thereafter and America's Palestine policy was not changed. Neither was the Arabs.

Chapter 3 Notes

1. P.R.O. Premier 4/51/9, 31 October 1939, pp. 1278-1279.

2. H. St. John Philby. <u>Note on Interview with Colonel Hoskins</u>, November 11, 1943. Philby Papers, St. Anthony's College, Oxford, (Hereafter listed as '<u>Note on Hoskins</u>')

3. British Legation (Jedda) reports for the months of February through December 1939, F.O. 371/24588.

4. Sir R. Bullard, Report on British Foreign Office, October 29, 1939. F.O. 371/24588 E 7604/2624/483/77.

5. Sir R. Bullard. Report to British Foreign Office, September 19, 1939. F.O. 371/24588.

6. Mr. Stonehewer-Bird to Viscount Halifax. Jedda, July 18, 1940, F.O. 371/24588.

7. Bullard. Jedda report for October 29, 1939.

8. Ibid. Ibn Saud declared he would give up his Kingdom if the people so desired.

9. Philby, "King Ibn Saud Speaks at Last", <u>Asia</u>. New York, Vol. 38, 1938, pp. 717-718.

10. United States, Department of State. Foreign Relations of the United States (Hereafter FRUS)., 1940, Vol. III, pp. 832-836.

11. Ibid., pp. 850-852.

12. V. Jabotinsky. <u>The Jewish War Front</u>. (London: 1940). Contains the "Jewish War Demands" of: a Jewish army, a world-Jewish civil authority, and a seat on any future Peace Conference; the Jewish State; a covenant on civic equality. States that Palestine must inevitably include Transjordan in order to obsorb the Jewish exodus.

13. Sir R. Bullard. Report to British Foreign Office. December 2, 1939. F.O. 371/24588 E 8086/2924/483/84. See also. Sir Reader Bullard, The Camels Must Go: An Autobiography. (London: Faber and Faber, 1961), pp. 200-206.

14. Philby. Asia.

15. Philby. Arabian Jubilee, (New York: John Day Co., 1953), p. 214.

16. Mr. Stonehewer-Bird to Viscount Halifax. Jedda Report for April 1940. F.O. 371/24588 E 1734/482/25.

17. Jedda message No. 26, March 4, 1940. F.O. 371/24588.

18. "Activities of Mr. Philby in Saudi Arabia." February 12 - June 14, 1940. F.O. 371/24589.

19. Ibid.

20. Philby. Note on Hoskins.

21. Ibid.

22. Elizabeth Monroe. Philby of Arabia. (London: Faber and Faber, 1973), p. 222.

23. FRUS. 1940, Vol. III, p. 840; and Chaim Weizmann. Trial and Error, an Autobiography, (New York: Schoken Books, 1966), p. 420, Reprint of London: Weizmann Foundation, 1949.

24. Philby. Arabian Jubilee, p. 214.

25. Monroe, pp. 222-223.

26. Philby. Note on Hoskins.

27. Stonehewer-Bird telegram to the Foreign Office. P.R.O.F.O. 371/24587 E 1963/710/25, message no. 146. July 12, 1940.

28. Elie Kedourie. _In the Anglo-Arab Labyrinth: The McMahon-Hussein Correspondence_. (New York: Cambridge University Press, 1976). A comprehensive study of the perceptions and misperceptions of intentions and promises exchanged in English and Arabic during World War I.

29. Stonehewer-Bird telegram, July 12, 1940.

30. Monroe, p. 228.

31. P.R.O.F.O. 371/24587. P.Z. 4310, 3 August 1940.

32. Monroe, p. 229.

33. P.R.O.F.O. 371/27270 E 269/269/25.

34. Monroe, p. 230.

35. _Summary of Events in Saudi Arabia During 1941_. Arabia. July 22, 1942. F.O. 371/27278 E 4326/4326/25.

36. F.R.U.S., 1941, Vol. III, pp. 624-651. A great deal of discussion occurred between the State Department, the Defense Department, the Federal Loan Administrator, the head of Lend-Lease and the White House. Arabian oil was not useable in the Navy's Fleet and America was not yet at war. Arabia was considered too far afield for America, it was within Britain's sphere of influence. By 1943 that would all change however.

37. F.O. 371/27278.

38. Ibid.

39. _New York Times_. December 30, 1940, p. 10:5. The Sherif's death sentence was commutted to life imprisonment. His chief aide, El Abet el Dib, was executed.

40. F.O. 371/27278. Ibn Saud sent his son, Abdul Aziz Sudairi, to Amman to clear the air. Gifts and expressions of mutual regard were exchanged.

41. Lenczowski., pp. 273-275. A more detailed account is presented by George Kirk. Survey of International Affairs 1939-1946: The Middle East in the War. (Londond: Oxford University Press, 1952), pp. 56-78.

42. Dr. Chaim Weizmann. Trial and Error, An Autobiography. (New York: Schocken Books, 1966), Reprint of London: Weizmann Foundation, 1949, p. 419.

43. Ibid.

44. Ibid., p. 420.

45. F.R.U.S., 1940. Vol. III, pp. 836-840. Dr. Weizmann met with President Roosevelt two days later.

46. He had previously spoken with Mr. Churchill and envisioned three to four million Jewish refugees in the future state.

47. F.R.U.S., 1940. Vol. III, p. 840.

48. Ibid.

49. Weizmann, p. 420.

50. Ibid., p. 425. He stated that he was sent by the British Government.

51. F.R.U.S., 1941. Vol. III, p. 600.

52. Ibid., pp. 598-599. The State Department wanted to speak with Dr. Weizmann personally but he was ill and a representative was sent. He was 68 years old at the time.

53. Weizmann, p. 425. A Jewish brigade was finally formed in the fall of 1944 and it joined the Allies in Italy in March 1945. Lenczowski, p. 398.

54. Ibid.

55. Philby, p. 215. Mention is made in a 1943 Foreign Office minute that indicated Philby had mentioned his plan to the Prime Minister's Private Secretary in 1941. Precise names and dates were not mentioned. F.O. 371/40139 E 3327/506/65, June 8, 1943.

56. E 7295/53/65.

57. Weizmann, p. 427.

58. Ibid., p. 428.

59. Meyer W. Weisgal. Ed., Chaim Weizmann: A Biography by Several Hands. (New York: Atheneum, 1963), p. 261. The biographers did not cite a specific source for their quote. The editor's note indicates that the Weizmann Archieves in Rehovoth provided much of the source material.

60. Philby, p. 215.

61. New York Times, April 15, 1942, 6:5. There are no indications that his trip was delayed in any way.

62. Weizmann, p. 428.

63. J. C. Hurewitz. Diplomacy in the Near and Middle East. A Documentary Record: 1914-1956, Vol. II. (New York: D. Van Norstrand Co., 1956), pp. 234-235.

64. Weisgal, p. 264.

65. J. C. Hurewitz. The Struggle for Palestine. (New York: Greenwood Press, 1968), pp. 159-164. The efforts of Dr. Judah L. Magnes, the American-born President of the Hebrew University, are

most notable. His opposition group formed the Union (<u>Ihud</u>) Association in September 44 and worked for a bi-national state which was to be part of a regional Federation of States. Under his plan the Arabs would have majority control. See his article in the January 1943 issue of <u>Foreign Affairs</u>. A detailed presentation of <u>pro</u> and <u>con</u> Jewish reactions may be found in the Esco Foundation for Palestine publication. <u>Palestine: A Study of Jewish, Arab, and British Policies</u>. (New Haven: Yale University Press, 1947), pp. 1078-1120.

66. Thomas A. Bryson. <u>Seeds of Mideast Crisis</u>. (Jefferson, North Carolina: McFarland Co., 1981), p. 69.

67. Ibid., pp. 550-551.

68. Ibid., pp. 553-556.

69. F.R.U.S., 1942. Vol. IV., pp. 24-36. America also dispatched an irrigation and agricultural mission headed by Mr. K. S. Twitchell who was in Saudi Arabia from May 10 to December 5, 1942. Ibid., pp. 561-567. During the same period overflight permission was granted and discussions on possible American Air Defense systems around the oil fields were conducted. Ibid., pp. 568-585. For an appreciation of the military activities as they related to political events see: Robert Goralski, <u>World War II Almanac: 1931-1945. A Political and Military Record</u>. (New York: Putnam, 1981).

70. F.R.U.S., 1943. Vol. IV., pp. 747-751.

71. Ibid., p. 751. Amir Faisal and Amir Khalid visited America in November 1943.

72. Ibid., pp. 757-763.

73. Ibid., p. 761.

74. Ibid., p. 762.

75. Ibid., pp. 768-771.

76. Ibid., pp. 788-789. The King considered publishing his 1938 letter to President Roosevelt; granting an interview with the Associated Press Correspondent, Clyde Farnsworth; and his subsequent April 1943 letter to the President seemed to be designed for public consumption also. Cordell Hull sent a polite message indicating that publishing the 1938 letter was not "well suited to American conditions. Ibid., p. 786.

77. Ibid., p. 770.

78. Ibid., p. 771.

79. Ibid., pp. 776-780. BG Hurley visited; French Morroco, Egypt, Palestine, Lebanon, Iraq and Syria.

80. Ibid., p. 778.

81. Ibid., p. 779. This attitude was the result of comments from Sir Ronald Storrs, former High Commissioner to Palestine, who told Auni Bey that His Majesty's Government was opposed to a Jewish State and maintained its adherence to the Balfour Declaration and the White Paper position on a Jewish National Home in Palestine but the United States was forcing the British to acquiesce. A rumor that was prevalent in Palestine related to a private conversation in Cairo where Churchill was allegedly to have said, "I am committed to the establishment of a Jewish State in Palestine and the President will accept nothing less.", Ibid.

82. Ibid., p. 778. See also Hurewitz, Diplomacy, pp. 236-237.

83. Ibid., pp. 781-785. I have included Ltc. Hoskins "Plan for Peace in the Near East" following his summary. It was obtained from Professor R. L. Greaves' copies of F.O. 371/34976 dated 20 March 1943.

84. F.R.U.S., 1943. Vol. IV., pp. 773-775.

85. Ibid., pp. 786-787.

86. Ibid., p. 788.

87. Noel Busch, "Life Visits Arabia," Life, May 31, 1943, pp. 76-77.

88. Report by Ltc. Hoskins. "King Ibn Saud - Man Not Myth," October 18, 1943, F.O. 371/34976, p. 4. Also F.R.U.S., 1943. Vol. IV, p. 809.

89. Mr. Jebb's memo of their meeting of 8 June, with attached minutes for 11-17 June 1943. F.O. 371/40139 E 3327/506/65.

90. Ibid. Two sets of initials are unreadable; the others were R.M.A. Hankey and C.W. Baxter; both were Foreign Office officials.

91. F.R.U.S., 1943. Vol. IV., pp. 792-794. Memorandum by Dr. Weizmann to British Foreign Office dated 12 June, which Ltc. Hoskins brought back from England in September, 1943. F.O. 371/35035 E 3648/87/31 dated June 24, 1943.

92. Ibid., p. 794. Dr. Weizmann's memo simply indicated that Hoskins was to "prepare the ground." Dr. Weizmann tried to block Hoskins selection and wanted Philby to go. See Weizmann letter to Welles at Appendix N and compare it with his memo.

93. Ibid., pp. 795-797. Contains Secretary of State (Hull's) correspondence with the British (12-29 June) and his instructions to Ltc. Hoskins (July 7). The British asked that Ltc. Hoskins make no suggestions involving territorial alterations and in no way prejudice the interests of other Arabs. His visit should also be as unobtrusive as possible.

94. Ibid., pp. 807-810.

95. Ibid., pp. 811-814. Memorandum of conversation by Ltc. Hoskins. The President's Holy Land trusteeship idea was pursued until it was realized that the Jews and Arabs would not reach an agreement on any solution. See memo by Merriam: Ibid., pp. 816-822 and George Kirk.

96. Ibid., p. 815.

97. F.O. 371/34976 E 7115/2551/65.

98. Weizmann, p. 432.

99. Ibid., p. 433.

100. Oliver Stanley memo on Dr. Weizmann's visit, August 31, 1943. F.O. 371/35038.

101. Paragraph 2 is also evidence that his meeting with Mr. Murray in 1940 was also an exercise in manipulation.

102. The extracts and revisions were determined by comparing Philby's copy from his personal papers and the enclosure entitled, "Extracts from a statement sent to me by Mr. St. John Philby, 17.11.43. attached to Dr. Weizmann's letter. F.O. 371/40139 E 206/206/31.

103. Ibid. The minuted comments were made by an officer of the North American Department whose signature is not discernable and by R. M. A. Hankey of the Foreign Office.

104. Weizmann, p. 436.

105. Kirk, p. 317.

106. Philby, pp. 216-217.

107. Thomas M. Campbell, ed., The Diaries of Edward R. Stettinius, Jr. 1943-1946. (New York: New Viewpoints, 1975), p. 174.

108. David Van Der Meulen. <u>The Wells of Ibn Saud</u>. (New York: Praeger, 1957), p. 157.

109. Ibid., p. 158.

110. Colonel William A. Eddy, <u>F.D.R. Meets Ibn Saud</u>. (New York: Middle East House, 1954), p. 30. Eddy was the first U.S. Minister to Saudi Arabia. His is the only record of the political discussion.

111. Ibid., p. 34.

112. Ibic.

113. Edward R. Stettinius, Jr. <u>Roosevelt and the Russians: The Yalta Conference.</u> (Garden City: Doubleday and Company, Inc., 1949), p. 289. The underlined words are my emphasis.

CONCLUSION

St. John Philby's plan for a solution to the Palestine problem was accepted by the Zionist leadership because it supported their objectives. Ibn Saud did not reject the plan in 1940. By the end of 1943 the conflicting interests of the various groups and personalities were such that it became a moot point. It continued to be an issue only because of the persistence of the Zionists and its author. St. John Philby and his plan were used as a means to achieve an end. The two enabled the Zionists to maintain a hope for a negotiated solution and they provided the basis for this study.

Philby's plan did not lead to a peaceful solution. Rather, it probably contributed to the perpetuation of President Roosevelt's false perception that Ibn Saud would help him to achieve the Zionist's objective. There is nothing to be gained by trying to surmise "what if" President Roosevelt came to the realization that America should have reviewed its Palestine policy in 1943, rather than shortly before his death in 1945. The purpose here is to summarize the conflicting interests and perceptions which precluded the acceptance of Philby's plan.

One of the major contributing factors to the failure of Philby's plan was Philby himself. St. John Philby saw himself as the herald of a King whose greatness was not yet recognized by the Great Powers. His motivation seems to have been simply a desire for fame. His plan was designed to place his King in the uppermost leadership position in the Arab world - with Philby at his side. Ambition and anti-British hostility, coupled with a total lack of tact, precluded the egocentric Arabist from being an effective mediator. The political interests of the Zionists were supported but the interests of the other parties concerned were not.

From an overall Arab perspective it was a negative plan. It would have established a Jewish State in a traditionally Arab land. A fundamentalist Wahhabi monarch was to be the overseer of the transfer of settled Mediterranean Sunni Muslims into either the predominately nomadic regions of Transjordan or into Iraq with its large percentage of Shiites. The establishment of a fixed price of £20,000,000 served as a simple cost figure for the Zionists but it did not readily represent a concern for the long term social and economic interests of the displaced Arabs.

The Zionist's objective was to establish a Jewish State in Palestine which would have economic influence in the region. Providing compensation for Arab land in Palestine in the form of land development work and Jewish goods would have served Jewish interests. Philby's plan was an additional means used to keep the hope for negotiation alive and the immigration door open. The Zionists were understandably concerned about the tragic plight of their co-religionists in Europe and desired a more secure future for them. Unfortunately the Arabs were not able to discern in the Zionist's actions a similar concern for their future.

Philby's plan also conflicted with the British interests. The British were not yet willing to relinquish their control over the region which protected their routes to India. Philby's personality also clashed with those of the professionals in the British Civil Service. His credentials were no longer valid and therefore any plan he was associated with would have been viewed with apprehension.

American interests were not yet clearly defined and the population/electorate was generally ignorant of all the facts associated with the Palestine problem. Therefore the approach taken was to look for a negotiated settlement which met as many of the demands from all parties as possible. The assessments given by BG Hurley and Ltc. Hopkins were not heeded while the prospect for a negotiated settlement was still believed to exist.

Ibn Saud was a wise ruler who maintained a consistent set of priorities and a moderate approach to the Palestine problem. His first concern was for the interests of his Kingdom and its people. He therefore avoided actions which would endanger the economic security he enjoyed with the British, while he developed alternative sources of income (oil) which would allow him greater latitude in regional politics. His main regional interest was the blocking of any growth in Hashimite power. His approach to the Palestine problem reflected his personal sincerity in believing that the Great Powers would not impose an unjust solution. When in 1945 the Zionist's progress portended fulfillment of their objective he contacted President Roosevelt and personally conveyed the Arab side of the problem. His position was consistently presented in his letters of 1938 and 1943, and in his Life interview. He believed that: the Jewish historical claim was fallacious, the Balfour Declaration was unjust because the British had no right to give away Arab land, Moslems could not accept the Jewish religious claim - they too were decendants of Abraham, Palestine was too small to accept the world Jewry and the Allies should accept their share of refugees. Further, he believed that

Zionist propaganda kept the world ignorant of the facts. His wisdom
kept him from being fanatical in his opposition and he chose the
moderate approach. To lead his people against the world's most powerful military forces would not have served their interests.

Philby's plan was one of the many being put forward in the course
of World War II. None of the plans overcame the irreconcilable
differences between the Arabs and the Jews. The search for a solution
to the Palestine problem was moved to the battlefield - with inconclusive results.

Appendix A: Proposed draft of Philby - Ben-Gurian Agreement,
May 26, 1937.

"We, the undersigned, are agreed on the following points:

1) During the Great War the British Government made certain
    promises to the Arabs in respect of the independence of all
    Arab territories and also promised to the Jews all necessary
    assistance in their efforts to establish a National Home
    in Palestine.

2) Logically these two sets of promises are incompatible with
    each other, and in practice they have resulted in the reduc-
    tion of Palestine to the status of a British Colony peopled
    by two equally dissatisfied races.

3) The existing impasse, resulting from the rebellion of 1936,
    is unlikely to be resolved by the recommendations of the
    Royal Commission, whose terms of reference debarred it from
    considering the Palestine problem from all angles.

4) Nothing indeed but a freely negotiated agreement between
    Arabs and Jews can provide a satisfactory or permanent
    solution of the problem.

5) The alternatives before the Jews are: a) to look to the
    West for support in the accomplishment of their dream; or
    b) to recognize their affinities with Arabia. From a) they
    have little to hope for, while b) is acceptable to them
    provided they can be guaranteed the position they seek in
    Palestine.

6) The Arabs demand the abrogation of the Mandate and the with-
    drawl of the Balfour Declaration. The Jews would not oppose
    this demand in return for a suitable agreement with the
    Arabs.

7) Both parties equally object to any partition of Palestine
    (as has been suggested) into Jewish, Arab and British spheres.
    Indeed, the Jews desire, and the Arabs favour, the extension
    of Palestine to form a single independent state with
    Transjordan, without internal religious barriers.

3) The Jews demand the unrestricted right of immigration for
    all persons of Jewish race who desire to become citizens of
    Palestine. The Arabs, subject to the acceptance of the
    principles stated in 5 and 7 above, would (or should) agree
    to allow immigration to all intending citizens of the
    Greater Palestine, without distinction of race or creed,
    subject only to the absorptive capacity of the country.

9) a) The capacity of the country to accept the resulting
influx of new citizens, greatly increased by the inclusion
of Transjordan, would be determined by a mixed ad hoc
permanent commission, subject to i) the Government, and
ii) arbitration by the Permanent Court of International
Justice, if necessary.

b) The Commission envisaged above might consist of a League
of Nations President, two Jews nominated by the Jewish
Agency, and two Arabs, together with a representative
of the Arab State or States guaranteeing the agreement.

10) a) The Jews would require guarantees for the faithful obser-
vance of any such agreement arrived at between them and
the Arabs.

b) Assuming the union of Palestine and Transjordan to form
a single political unit under an indigenous Government,
the guarantee would be given by that Government. This
guarantee would be confirmed by the countersignature
i) of the League of Nations, ii) of one or all of the
other independent Arab States, who would in the first
instance be specially responsible to enforce the local
Government's guarantee--a Commission representing these
Arab States might in fact be the special immigration
commission envisaged in 9. In the last resort, the
League of Nations would be responsible to intervene.

c) A possible solution would be to place the Greater Palestine under the protection of Ibn Saud alone, as the most
likely Power to be able to enforce the guarantee, in
which case the League of Nations would have no actual
responsibility in practice.

d) The form of the future Government of the Greater Palestine
would be for a plebiscite to determine, e.g., monarchy
under Emir Abdullah or some other monarch, or republic
with a periodically elected President.

e) No Power, other than the various Arab States of the
Peninsula, would be allowed any kind of preferential
treatment, in the Greater Palestine--whether strategic,
commercial or economic.

11) The Jews would, of course, be guaranteed complete freedom
to lead their religious and cultural lives according to their
own principles."

Source: David Ben-Gurian, *My Talks with Arab Leaders*, Jerusalem, 1922.

Appendix B: Letter of Ben-Gurion to H. St. John Philby, May 31, 1937.

<u>"Personal</u>   London
                                                         31st May, 1937.

H. St. John Philby, Esq., C.I.E.
18 Acol Street, N.W.

Dear Mr. Philby,

    As promised when we met, I am sending you my own personal
observations on your draft agreement.

    It seems that we are agreed that the recommendations of the Royal
Commission may be expected to satisfy neither Jews nor Arabs, and
that a satisfactory and enduring solution can best be reached by a
free agreement between Jews and Arabs. There is also no difference
of opinion between us with regard to the partition scheme: we both
feel that we have to oppose not only the partition rumoured to be
contemplated by the Royal Commission, but also to try and make good
the mistake made by the separation of Palestine from Transjordan, and
to re-unite the two halves of Palestine into a single economic and
political unit. We are also agreed that Jewish immigration should be
regulated in accordance with the economic absorptive capacity of the
country, and that a guarantee of the League of Nations is necessary
to ensure the rights of Jewish immigration. We agree, too, that
Palestine should be completely independent, so far, at least, as her
internal affairs are concerned. Jews and Arabs should be free to
arrange for their cultural and religious needs in their own way.

    The central idea of our proposals is a free agreement between
Jews and Arabs for a united Palestine. But I feel bound to point out
that in your proposals the essential condition of such an agreement
is missing. Your opposition to the probable findings of the Royal
Commission is based - and here I agree with you - on the assumption
that they will satisfy neither side; but if we want to reach any
agreement between Jews and Arabs, this is impossible unless both
parties obtain the satisfaction of their principal rights and claims.
While your suggestion would, I think, give complete satisfaction to
the Arabs - abolition of the Balfour Declaration, termination of the
Mandate, independence of Palestine, it ignores completely the rights
and claims of the Jews. You recognise in practice, it is true,
the principle of immigration, but only in the form of general
immigration; you do not discriminate against Jewish immigration, but
you show no recognition of the fact that Jewish immigration to
Palestine is as of right, and is a result of the Jewish people's
rights in Palestine, and of their historical connection with Palestine.
No agreement is conceivable which does not explicitly recognise the
right of the Jewish people to establish themselves in Palestine. The
Jews coming to Palestine do not regard themselves as immigrants:
they are returning as of right to their own historic homeland. This
right is limited only by the condition that the Palestine Arabs shall

not be displaced. We are fully ready to admit this limitation;
but you will not find a single Jew who would consent to the abolition
of the Mandate in favour of an agreement with the Arabs which
contained no clear recognition of the right of the Jews to enter
Palestine and re-establish there their National Home. We are not
intruders in Palestine, and our right to immigrate cannot be regarded
as only a part of the general right of immigration into the country
by "all intending citizens."

Moreover, there is in fact no immigration problem for any of the
Arab peoples. The territories held by independent and semi-independent
Arab States would provide for a much larger population than they
at present possess. Palestine is not, essentially, a country of
immigration; before the war thousands of Arabs emigrated annually
from it. Palestine is not capable of absorbing large additional
immigration except through the methods adopted by the Jews, i.e.,
the expenditure of large sumes of capital and much enterprise on the
improvement of the soil, irrigation, the creation of new industries,
etc. It is unreasonable to expect this expenditure of capital and
energy to continue if it is to provide for an immigration from all
over the world - Italian, Slav, Arab, Turkish - in which possibly
a few Jews may be included.

Thus, without this basis of recognition of the Jewish right to
enter Palestine, there can be no agreement. And it is not only an
abstract recognition of the principle which is necessary, but practical
and effective guarantees that our immigration will not be interfered
with so long as it does not exceed the economic absorptive capacity
of the country.

In my view, this can only be done by the regulation of Jewish
immigration by the Jewish Agency itself, subject to the supervision
of the Palestine Government, and to the submission of any disputes
arising between the Agency and the Government to arbitration and
decision by the League of Nations. It will be for the Government
to see that Jewish immigration does not exceed the absorptive capacity
of the country, but the final decision must rest with the League of
Nations, either through a special representative for this purpose
in Palestine, or through some other suitable means.

Your proposal in para. 9 would in practice hand over the control
of immigration to the Arabs, more especially since the Government
itself, particularly after the re-integration of Transjordan into
Palestine, will consist, in the great majority, of Arabs.

Another problem which is of vital importance for us is the
question of the constitutional regime in Palestine itself. At our
first meeting, you expressed apprehension that the continuation of
Jewish immigration would in a short time make Palestine into a Jewish
State, since the Jews would, in 10 or 12 years, become a majority
there. I quite understand this apprehension. The Arabs are entitled
to be guaranteed against domination by the Jews. But the Jews are
also entitled to be guaranteed against domination by the Arabs. In

my views, the only way to achieve these guarantees is the establishment of complete parity, as between Jews and Arabs, irrespective of their numbers, in all central organs of the Palestine Government. I hope that this agreement will not be necessary for ever, because I believe that the time will come when Arabs and Jews will work together in mutual confidence, and the lines of devision will become other than radical ones. This consciousness of a common citizenship will develop gradually as a result of economic cooperation, but until it has developed, and until the present racial suspiciousness has disappeared, it is necessary to have some arrangement which will prevent either race from being dominated by the other.

It now remains for me to add a few secondary observations.

(a) The statement in para. 1 of your memorandum is not wholly in agreement with the facts, so far as they are known to me. The promises made to the Arabs did not include the independence of all Arab territories. Palestine and part of Syria were expressly excluded. I also do not believe that the promises made to the Arabs were incompatible with the promise made to the Jews. On the other hand, the Mandate expressly recognizes the historical connection of the Jewish people with Palestine, and whatever may be our different views on this point, I think it is unnecessary to include these controversial questions, which have a mainly historical value, in an agreement of this kind.

(b) I cannot subscribe to para. 3 as it stands, although I too believe that the Commission will not succeed in satisfying either party, though my reasons may perhaps not be the same as your own.

(c) In the phrasing of para. 5 I think "Jewish dream" is hardly the right word. There are now in Palestine more than 400,000 Jews, and with our achievements in the country, and a population of this size, it is hardly possible to speak of Zionism as a "dream".

(d) As regards para. 10, I would observe that, if and when the Mandate is abolished, it will be necessary to replace it not only by a guarantee from the Arab peoples, but also by a guarantee from the League of Nations. I do not place too high hopes in the latter institution, but so far, there is no better instrument or organised world opinion. The League of Nations includes among its members two Arab States.

Finally, I also doubt whether the complete exclusion of Gt. Britain from this agreement would be desirable or feasible. The Jews will certainly do nothing behind the back of Gt. Britain. Palestine should be independent; but in my view, a Jewish-Arab agreement is in practice impossible without the consent and approval of Gt. Britain. And such consent is hardly imaginable without due recognition of the vital interests of Gt. Britain in Palestine - of course without prejudice to the real independence of the Palestinian State.

With kind regards, I am,

Yours sincerely,

D.B.G."

Source: The Central Zionist Archievs. Jerusalem, File S25/10095.

Appendix C: Peel Com-
        mission Partition Plan

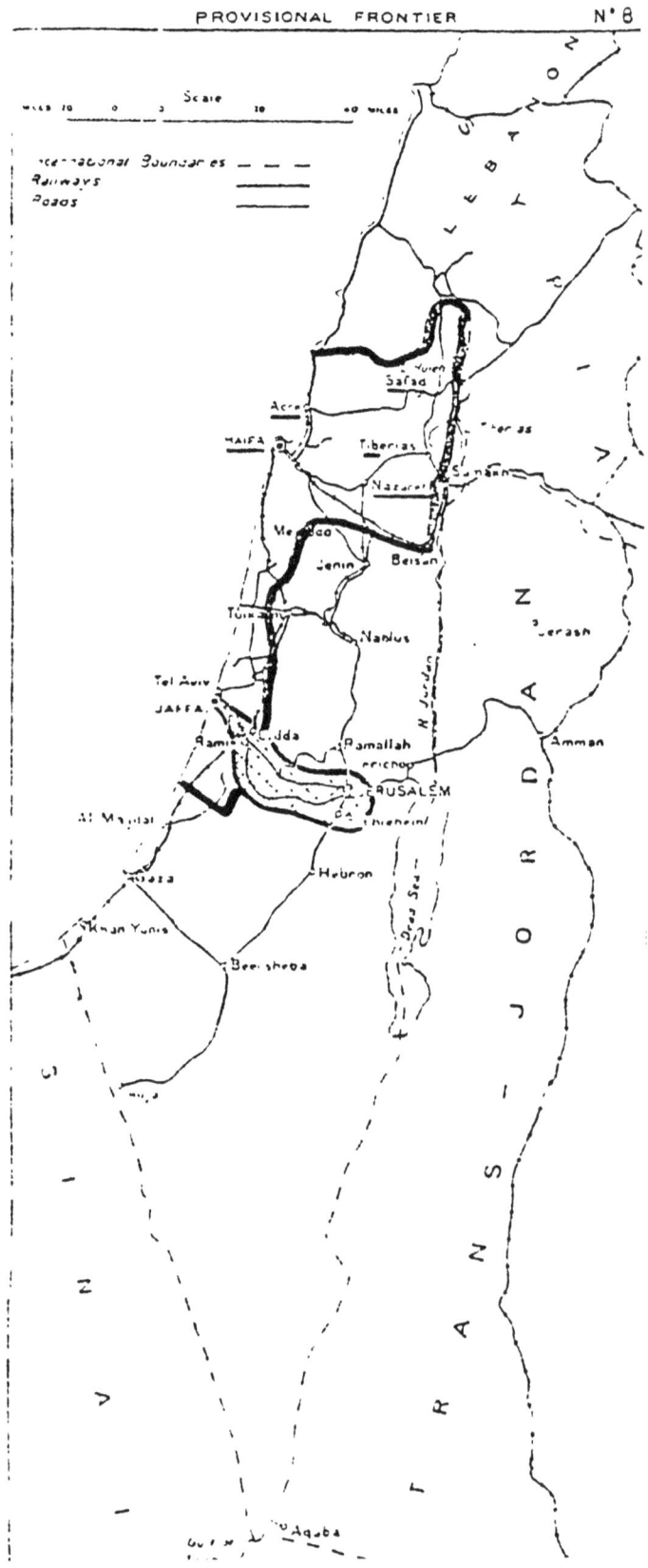

Source: Great Britain.
    Parliamentary Papers.
    Command (Cmd) 5479
    Palestine Royal Com-
    mission Report, 1937.

Appendix D: Palestine Royal Commission (Peel) Report, Conclusion, 1937.

"I. "Half a loaf is better than no bread" is a peculiarly
English proverb; and, considering the attitude which both the Arab
and the Jewish representatives adopted in giving evidence before us,
we think it improbable that either party will be satisfied at first
sight with the proposals we have submitted for the adjustment of their
rival claims. For Partition means that neither will get all it wants.
It means that the Arabs must acquiesce in the exclusion from their
sovereignty of a piece of territory, long occupied and once ruled by
them. It means that the Jews must be content with less than the Land
of Israel they once ruled and have hoped to rule again. But it seems
to us possible that on reflection both parties will come to realize
that the drawbacks of Partition are outweighed by its advantages.
For, if it offers neither party all it wants, if offers each what it
wants most, namely freedom and security.

2. The advantages to the Arabs of Partition on the lines we
have proposed may be summarized as follows:--

(i)   They obtain their national independence and can cooperate
        on an equal footing with the Arabs of the neighbouring
        countries in the cause of Arab unity and progress.

(ii)   They are finally delivered from the fear of being "swamped"
        by the Jews and from the possibility of ultimate subjection
        to Jewish rule.

(iii)   In particular, the final limitation of the Jewish National
        Home within a fixed frontier and the enactment of a new
        Mandate for the protection of the Holy Places, solemnly
        guaranteed by the League of Nations, removes all anxiety
        lest the Holy Places should ever come under Jewish control.

(iv)   As a set-off to the loss of territory the Arabs regard as
        theirs, the Arab State will receive a subvention from the
        Jewish State. It will also, in view of the backwardness
        of Trans-Jordan, obtain a grant of £2,000,000 from the
        British Treasury; and, if an arrangement can be made for
        the exchange of land and population, a further grant will be
        made for the conversion, as far as may prove possible, of
        uncultivable land in the Arab State into productive land
        from which the cultivators and the State alike will profit.

3. The advantages of Partition to the Jews may be summarized
as follows:--

(i)   Partition secures the establishment of the Jewish National
        Home and relieves it from the possibility of its being
        subjected in the future to Arab rule.

(ii) Partition enables the Jews in the fullest sense to call their National Home their own: for it converts it into a Jewish State. Its citizens will be able to admit as many Jews into it as they themselves believe can be absorbed. They will attain the primary objective of Zionism--a Jewish nation, planted in Palestine, giving its nationals the same status in the world as other nations give theirs. They will cease at last to live a "minority life."

4. To both Arabs and the Jews Partition offers a prospect--and we see no such prospect in any other policy--of obtaining the inestimable boon of peace. It is surely worth some sacrifice on both sides if the quarrel which the Mandate started could be ended with its termination. It is not a natural or old-standing feud. An able Arab exponent of the Arab case told us that the Arabs throughout their history have not only been free from anti-Jewish sentiment but have also shown that the spirit of compromise is deeply rooted in their life. And he went on to express his sympathy with the fate of the Jews in Europe. "There is no decent-minded person," he said, "who would not want to do everything humanly possible to relieve the distress of those persons," provided that it was "not at the cost of inflicting a corresponding distress on another people." Considering what the possibility of finding a refuge in Palestine means to many thousands of suffering Jews, we cannot believe that the "distress" occasioned by Partition, great as it would be, is more than Arab generosity can bear. And in this, as in so much else connected with Palestine, it is not only the peoples of that country that have to be considered. The Jewish Problem is not the least of the many problems which are disturbing international relations at this critical time and obstructing the path to peace and prosperity. If the Arabs at some sacrifice could help to solve that problem, they would earn the gratitude not of the Jews alone but of all the Western World.

5. There was a time when Arab statesmen were willing to concede little Palestine to the Jews, provided that the rest of Arab Asia were free. That condition was not fulfilled then, but it is on the eve of fulfillment now. In less than three years' time all the wide Arab area outside Palestine between the Mediterranean and the Indian Ocean will be independent, and, if Partition is adopted, the greater part of Palestine will be independent too.

6. There is no need to stress the advantage to the British people of a settlement in Palestine. We are bound to honour to the utmost of our power the obligations we undertook in the exigencies of war towards the Arabs and the Jews. When those obligations were incorporated in the Mandate, we did not fully realize the difficulties of the task it laid on us. We have tried to overcome them, not always with success. They have steadily become greater till now they seem almost insuperable. Partition offers a possibility of finding a way through them, a possibility of obtaining a final solution of the problem which does justice to the rights and aspirations of both the Arabs and the Jews and discharges the obliga-

tions we undertook towards them twenty years ago to the fullest extent that is practicable in the circumstances of the present time.

7. Nor is it only the British people, nor only the nations which conferred the Mandate or approved it, who are troubled by what has happened and is happening in Palestine. Numberless men and women all over the world would feel a sense of deep relief if somehow an end could be put to strife and bloodshed in a thrice hallowed land.

ALL OF WHICH WE HUMBLY SUBMIT FOR YOUR
MAJESTY'S GRACIOUS CONSIDERATION

J. M. MARTIN,
    Secretary.
22nd June, 1937.

PEEL.
HORACE RUMBOLD.
LAURIE HAMMOND.
Wm. MORRIS CARTER.
HAROLD MORRIS.
R. COUPLAND."

Source: Great Britain, Parliamentary Papers, 1936-1937. Command
         Paper (Cmd) 5479, pp. 394-397, July 1937.

Appendix E: The King of Saudi Arabia (Abdul Es Saud) to President
            Roosevelt, November 29, 1933.

    "Mr. President: We have been informed of what has been published
regarding the position of the Government of the United States of
America concerning support of the Jews in Palestine. In view of
our confidence in your love of right and justice, and the attachment
of the free American People to the fundamental democratic traditions
based upon the maintenance of right and justice and succor for defeated peoples, and in view of the friendly relations existing
between our Kingdom and the Government of the United States, we wish
to draw your attention, Mr. President, to the cause of the Arabs in
Palestine and their legitimate rights, and we have full confidence
that our statement will make clear to you and the American People
the just cause of the Arabs in those Holy Lands.

    It has appeared to us from the account which has been published
of the American position that the case of Palestine has been considered from a single point of view: the point of view of the Zionist
Jews; and the Arab points of view have been neglected. We have
observed as one of the effects of the widespread Jewish propaganda
that the democratic American People has been grossly misled, and
it has resulted in considering support for the Jews in crushing the
Arabs in Palestine as an act of humanity. Although such an action
is a wrong directed against a peaceful people dwelling in their
country, they have not ceased to have confidence in the fairness of
general democratic opinion in the world at large and in America
particularly. I am confident that if the rights of the Arabs in
Palestine were clear to you, Mr. President, and the the American
People, you would give them full support.

    The argument on which the Jews depend in their claims regarding
Palestine is that they settled there for a time in the olden days
and that they have wandered in various countries of the world, and
that they wish to create a gathering-place for themselves in Palestine
where they may live freely. And for their action they rely upon a
promise they received from the British Government, namely: the
Balfour Declaration.

    As for the historical claim of the Jews, there is nothing to
justify it, because Palestine was and has not ceased to be occupied
by the Arabs through all the periods and progression of history,
and its sovereign was their sovereign. If we except the interval
when the Jews were established there, and a second period when the
Roman Empire ruled there, the ruler of the Arabs has been the ruler
of Palestine from the oldest times to our own day. The Arabs, through
the entire course of their existence have been the keepers of the
Holy Places, the magnifiers of their situation, the respecters of
their sanctity, maintaining their affairs with all faithfulness and
devotion. When the Ottoman Government extended over Palestine, Arab
influence was dominant, and the Arabs never felt that the Turks
were a colonizing power in their country, owing to:

1. The oneness of the religious bond;
2. The feeling of the Arabs that they were partners of the Turks in government;
3. The local administration of government being in the hands of the sons of the land itself.

From the foregoing it is seen that the Jewish claim of rights in Palestine in so far as it rests upon history has no reality, for if the Jews dwelt in Palestine for a certain period as possessors, surely the Arabs have dwelt there a far longer time, and it is impossible to consider the annexation of a country by a people as a natural right justifying their claim thereto. If this principle be now held in esteem, then it is the right of every people to reclaim the country it formerly occupied by force for a certain time. This would bring about astonishing changes in the map of the world, and would be irreconcilable with right, with justice, or with equity.

Now regarding the other cliam of the Jews, they take unto themselves the sympathy of the world because they are scattered and persecuted in various countries, and they would like to find a place in which to take shelter in order to be safe from the injustice they encounter in many countries.

The important thing in this matter is to discriminate between the cause of Judaism and Islam [*anti-Semitism*] in the world, as contrasted with the canse of political Zionism. The intention was sympathy for scattered Jews. But Palestine is a small country. It has already received such a great number of them as to exceed comparison with any country in the world, taking account of the limited area of Palestine as compared with the lands of the eartn where tne Jews dwell. There is no power to remedy the straitness of Palestine in order to make room for all the Jews of the world, even supposing it were empty of its inhabitants, the Arabs (as Mr. Malcolm MacDonald said in a speech which he delivered recently in the British House of Commons). If the principle be accepted that the Jews now in Palestine are to remain there, then that little country has already performed a greater human justice than any other. You will see, Mr. President, that it is not just that the governments of the worla-- including the United States--have closed their doors against the immigration of the Jews and impose on Palestine, a small Arab country, the task of sustaining them.

But if we look at the matter from the standpoint of political Zionism this point of view resembles [*represents*] a wrong and unjust way. Its aim is to ruin a peaceable and tranquil people and to drive them from their country by various means, and to feed the political greed and personal ambition of a few Zionists. As to the reliance of the Jews upon the Balfour Declaration, surely that Declaration has brought the limit of oppression and iniquity to a peaceful and tranquil country. It was given by a government which at the time of the gift did not possess the right to impose it upon Palestine. Similarly, the opinion of the Arabs of Palestine was not taken in this regard nor with regard to the arrangement of the Mandate which was imposed upon them, as has been made clear also by Malcolm MacDonald, British Minister of Colonies, and this in spite of promises given by the Allies, including America, that they would have the right of self-determination. It is important for us to mention that Balfour's promise was preceded by another promise from the British Government with the knowledge of the Allies regarding the rights of the Arabs in Palestine and in other Arab countries.

From this it will be clear to you, Mr. President, that the historical pretext of the Jews is unjust and it is impossible to consider it. Their plea from the standpoint of humanity has been fulfilled more by Palestine than by any other country, and Balfour's promise on which they depend is contrary to right and justice and inconsistent with the principle of self-determination. The ambition of the Zionists renders the Arabs in all countries apprehensive, and causes them to resist it.

The rights of the Arabs in Palestine do not admit of discussion because Palestine has been their country since the oldest times, and they did not leave it nor did others drive them out. Places flourished there, Arab in civilization, to an extent calling for admiration, for the reason that they were Arab in origin, in language, in situation, in culture; and of this there is no uncertainty or doubt. The history of the Arabs is full of just laws and useful works.

When the World War broke out, the Arabs sided with the Allies hoping to obtain their independence, and they were wholly confident that they would achieve it after the World War for the following reasons:

1. Because they participated in the War by action, and sacrificed their lives and property;
2. Because it was promised them by the British Government through notes exchanged between its representative at the time, Sir Henry McMahon, and the Sherif Hussein;
3. Because of your predecessor, the Great President Wilson who decided upon the participation of the United States of America in the War on the side of the Allies in support of high human principles, of which the most important was the right of self-determination;
4. Because the Allies declared in November 1919 [*1918*], following their occupation of the countries, that they entered them in order to free them and to give the people their liberty and independence.

Mr. President, if you will refer to the report submitted by the Commission of Investigation which your predecessor, President Wilson, sent to the Near East in 1919, you will find the demands which the Arabs in Palestine and Syria made when they were questioned as to what future they asked for themselves.

But unfortunately the Arabs found after the War that they were abandoned, and the assurances given did not materialize. Their lands have been divided and distributed unjustly. Artificial frontiers resulted from these divisions which are not justified by the facts of geography, nationality, or religion. In addition to this, they found themselves facing a very great danger: the incursion upon them of the Zionists, who became the possessors of their best lands.

The Arabs protested strongly when they learned of the Balfour Declaration, and they protested against the organization of the Mandate. They announced their rejection and their non-acceptance from the first day. The stream of Jewish immigration from various countries to Palestine has caused the Arabs to fear for their lives and their destiny; consequently numerous outbreaks and disturbances in Palestine took place in 1920, 1921, and 1929, but the most important outbreak was that of 1936, and its fire has not ceased to blaze to this hour.

Mr. President, the Arabs of Palestine and behind them the rest of the Arabs--or rather, the rest of the Islamic World--demand their rights, and they defend their lands against those who intrude upon them and their territories. It is impossible to establish peace in Palestine unless the Arabs obtain their rights, and unless they are sure that their countries will not be given to an alien people whose principles, aims and customs differ from theirs in every way. Therefore we beseech and adjure you Mr. President, in the name of Justice and Freedom and help for weak peoples for which the noble American People is celebrated, to have the goodness to consider the cause of the Arabs in Palestine, and to support those who live in peace and quiet despite attack from these homeless groups from all parts of the world. For it is not just that the Jews be sent away from all the various countries of the world and that weak, conquered Palestine should, against its will, suffer this whole people. We do not doubt that the high principles to which the American People adhere, will cause them to yield to right and grant support for justice and fair play.

Written in our Palace at Ar Riad on the seventh day of the month of Shawal, in the year 1357 of the Hejira, corresponding to November 29, 1938, A.D."

ABDUL AZIZ ES SAUD

Source: Foreign Relations of the United States, 1938. Vol. II, pp. 994-998.

152

Appendix F: Philby's interview of Ibn Saud, December 1938.

"On Sunday, August 7, the Arab world was electrified by the broadcast announcement that the Secretary of State for the Colonies had paid a surprise visit by air to Jerusalem and had already departed on his return to England. During the bare twenty-four hours of his stay he had seen the sights of the Holy Land by air and by car, and had sat in conference with the High Commissioner, the General Officer commanding the troops in Palestine and other high officials. The dramatic appearance and disappearance of the *deus ex machina* portended good or evil--no one knew which.

A notice was issued by the Broadcasting Station at Ramallah that the High Commissioner would be on the air the next evening at eight o'clock. Arabia tuned in--every receiver in the country was listening in. The moment arrived. *Parturiunt montes nascetur ridiculus mus.* Sir Harold MacMichael spoke--he sounded suitably emotional--for barely two minutes, and in those two minutes he delivered himself of platitude after platitude like a child repeating a lesson in class. At Riyadh the feeling was one of disappointment and of irritation that such an occasion had been used to repeat sentiments bordering on the burlesque.

I had had frequent opportunities of discussing Arab affairs in general and the present situation in particular with His Majesty King Ibn Saud, but His Majesty had in general evaded any statement of his sentiments for publication and I had refrained from any precise definition of his views and policy. I accordingly seized the opportunity of ascertaining something of his opinions with a view to publication--relying on my long-standing friendship with His Majesty and on his knowledge of my constant efforts in furthering Arab interests.

I began by explaining to His Majesty the sentiments I had heard expressed by various individuals and the trend of various articles I had read in the European and Arabic papers. I suggested the general astonishment of the public at the studied silence he had adopted in regard to the present situation and recent events in various Arab countries. His Majesty replied to all this in the following words: "I have considered that in present circumstances silence is the wisest course. In arriving at the conclusion I have put my trust in God and my reliance on the knowledge of all intelligent folk in Islam, and among the Arabs, of the deep sincerity of my religious and national convictions. That is one reason, and another is that I have not thought the circumstances suitable for the expression of my views.

"The present situation," I persisted, "demands an expression of your views so that the world may know them. Can your Majesty explain more clearly the reason of your silence and unwillingness to speak at the present time when every one concerned with the Arab cause is deeply concerned to know Your Majesty's opinion." I added: "Your Majesty is fully aware of your position in the Arab world and you know also how the British government respects your sentiments and acknowledges your status in Islam and Arabia. As your friend, it would not be backward in according favorable consideration of your views if you explained matters and communicated your opinions to it. On the other hand, you see the Arabs and Islam greatly exercised by affairs in Palestine, while many of them regret and criticize your silence."

His Majesty replied: "There is no doubt indeed of the friendship of Great Britain. The policy we have adopted in our political discussions with Britain and other powers is to treat all our conversations as confidential until we have disposed of the difficulties under consideration. I am satisfied that I have never failed to offer advice when I believed that the advice I had to offer was in the mutual interests of the English and the Arabs. Now I have offered such advice in the clearest terms and expressed my opinions to Great Britain regarding the present situation and the consequences that may be expected from the present policy she is following."

"That," I interrupted, "is certainly praiseworthy, but what is more important is that the world should know your opinions and that you yourself should be informed as to the reaction of Great Britain to your advice and representations."

His Majesty replied: "There are three reasons which lead me to think that the time is not ripe for such a public utterance. Firstly, because England is the friend of the Arabs and of all nations the one most needful of conciliating the Arabs and according to them their rights in view of the need for protecting her own interests and communications. Secondly, because between England and the Arabs there exist covenants and agreements as everybody knows. And, thirdly, because the present state of affairs and its consequences are not concealed from Great Britain, while, if the British government is weighing the matter as it deserves to be weighed and is actively considering it, then there is still nope that it will reconsider its position and take action in a manner consonant with its own interests and the interests of its Muslim and Arab friends, thus returning to the more reasonable course. But, if Britain has other objectives in view, then it seems to me that the words are of no use whatever if she has made up her mind and has determined to pursue such a course."

After a request from me that he should express an opinion as regards the advisability of keeping at any rate the Arabs advised of his views, His Majesty pursued: "God by praised, the Arabs understand well enough where I stand. They know me as the champion of their faith and race, but of a truth I do not see much advantage in giving expression to my sentiments and advice under present conditions. I have no desire to speak mor. precisely on this subject. Nevertheless, in view of the subtlety of the problem and fearing that my words may be interpreted in a manner which does not represent my views, I will give you a partial answer to your question. My advice to the Arabs from the beginning of my reign--and you know the Arabs are naturally intelligent as well as courageous and noble-minded--has been that they should be united both to defend their common interests and to give added weight to their status abroad. To this day, unfortunately, my hopes and wishes have in no way been realized. Most of the Arabs pursue their courses independently, though the aim and objective of all are identical. This plurality of ideas has certainly caused a setting-back of progress toward the desired goal. Talk without complete agreement and absolute confidence cannot produce the desired results. So when I saw this divergence of ideas I fell back upon myself and remained content to express my personal opinions only to those who referred to me or asked me my views on matters of concern to Arabia and Islam."

"I am given to understand," I said, "from the opinions I have heard expressed by Arabs and their chief leaders that Your Majesty's opinion is that which counts the highest in their view. I feel I am not far wrong in believing that they would in no way ignore your advice and guidance."

"That of course is true enough," replied His Majesty; "I myself do not doubt it for a moment, but all the same I have faith in the words of the poet,
   'Wisdom consists of acting only when the consequences of
   your act you clearly ken.'
My instinctive nature is such that before entering upon any matter I always look round to make sure that there is an exit as well as an entrance."

I thanked His Majesty for his clear explanation of many matters regarding which I had been in the dark. I craved, however, his permission to put him a specific question regarding Palestine--namely, the Jews' justification of their position in that country. His Majesty replied that he preferred not to make any comment on that issue, but I insisted that England believed herself to have made promises to the Jews in the Balfour Declaration, just as she had also made promises to the Arabs. His Majesty laughed and was silent. "I do not wish," he said at last, "to answer you on that point." I insisted, "It is the point on which the English rely."

"Glory be to God," he said at last, "that did not appoint a distant mark for the marksman! The Balfour promise was indeed the greatest injustice of Great Britain. Is it possible to imagine a greater calamity than taking away the lands and dwellings of the Arabs forcibly and handing them over to others? Why does Europe criticize Germany and others for turning out the Jews from their countries in which they are a minority in German, or other, territory and not find fault with herself, Europe, for scheming to turn the Arabs out of their country in order that the Jews may dwell therein? Admitting the British promises to the Arabs and the British Covenant with them--after all they did not give the Arabs any new property, they did not give them anything more than their own lands, their dwellings and the dwellings of their fathers and forefathers before them. The Arabs have been domiciled in these territories, which they conquered from the Romans, for hundreds of years in unchallenged

proprietary right. So how can there be a question of comparing one
set of promises with the other?"

"If this is then Your Majesty's opinion," I said, "Why do you
not advise the English accordingly?"

"I can assure you," he replied, "that these matters are not
hidden. England knows her own interests best. We have not failed to
inform her of what is in our minds."

I asked His Majesty whether in his opinion the recent visit of
the Colonial Secretary to Jerusalem portended any change or modification of policy. "I don't see anything strange in that," replied the
King. "Why should he not visit a country for whose administration
he is responsible, to see and satisfy himself about what is going
on therein?"

I then asked His Majesty if he would tell me what would be his
attitude if Great Britain decided in favor of partition and actually
set up a Jewish State and invited him to accord recognition thereto.
"The answer to that question," replied His Majesty, "is very simple
and quite obvious. The Arabs are many, and Islam is multiple. Now,
if the Arabs decline to recognize the Jewish State, then I would
obviously be with them and of them. And, if they were united in
agreeing to such recognition, then I would remain alone in my view.
And everybody knows full well that such action would not be consistent
with my religion nor would it be to the interests of the situation
in which I find myself."

"One more question!" I pleaded as His Majesty showed signs of
wishing to terminate the interview. "Can Your Majesty offer any
suggestion for a solution of the Palestine problem?" And His Majesty
answered: "I have already given you my views in the course of this
talk. And, if there is anything new in what I have said from which
the English and the Arabs may derive satisfaction, ther the time for
discussing it will arrive in due course."

The interview then terminated. So far as possible I have given
the King's views in his own words. And I have his permission to
make them public if I think they would be of interest to the world.
The fact that His Majesty's views, already well known enough to the
British government, have never yet been published gives added
importance to the breaking of his studied silence at what is a
supremely critical moment.

Source: Asia, December 1938, pp. 717-718.

Appendix G: Memorandum by Professor L.B. Namier, October 6, 1939.

"On Friday, October 6th, 1939, Dr. Weizmann, Mr. Shertok, and myself lunched with Mr. Philby.

Mr. Philby's scheme for settling the Arab-Jewish problem was discussed on the previous lines, and in greater detail. Philby's idea was that Western Palestine should be handed over completely to the Jews, clear of Arab population except for a "Vatican City" in the old city of Jerusalem. In return, the Jews should try to secure for the Arabs national unity and independence as, according to him, was promised in the MacMahon-Husse'n Correspondence; moreover, extensive financial help should be given to the Arabs by the Jews. Such unity could be achieved under Ibn Saud alone. Philby enviseges in the first place the handing over to Saudi Arabia of Syria and various small states on the Red Sea. He and his friends seem to be haunted by the fear of further Turkish encroachments in Syria and possibly Mosul. He did not clearly define what the future relations should be of Ibn Saud to Transjordan and Iraq, but thought that if all Arab States were granted full independence, a proper settlement would be reached.

Dr. Weizmann clearly emphasized that while we could promise economic advantages which would merely depend on us ourselves, we could not give any valid promises in the political sphere where we had not the power "to deliver the goods"; moreover, that we could not do anything which might conflict with our loyalty towards Great Britain and France. Still there were three very important factors inherent in the situation, which would favour a real settlement:

1. British public opinion would certainly back a reasonable claim for a Jewish-Arab settlement, and even be prepared to make certain sacrifices to achieve it.

2. Very influential American support for such a settlement can be expected.

3. The world will be faced at the end of the war with a very serious Jewish problem - of Jewish populations being evacuated from East European countries; and the man who could supply a possible solution for this problem would have a considerable claim on the world for benefits in return.

Dr. Weizmann said that when in America he expected to see President Roosevelt and to gain his support for some big scheme of such a character. If Mr. Philby meantime gained Ibn Saud's assent and support for his ideas, he should send word to me through the Saudi Arabian Legation in London, and I would transmit the message to Dr. Weizmann in America.

Philby was quite frank about the financial difficulties of Ibn Saud, increased as they are by the stoppage of pilgrimages during the war. He suggested the sum of £20,000,000 for Ibn Saud in case the scheme was carried out in full. Shertok suggested that part at least of that sum should be used for development in connection with the transfer of the Palestine Arabs to other Arab countries; and I emphasised that such sums could not be expected in specie, but in goods; e.g. if Ibn Saud requires arms - and this was one of the main items talked of by Philby - we could, over a certain period of time, supply them from Jewish armarment works in Palestine. Philby entirely agreed that such a subsidy would have to be distributed over a number of years, and paid, to a very large extent, in the form of goods.

After Weizmann and Shertok had left, I once more emphasised to Philby that while we were not in a position to make binding political promises about things not under our control, they and we alike had to put our faith in creating circumstances which would favour such a scheme; that in history it mattered most what it was "the stars worked for in their courses," and that any real settlement between the Jews and Arabs in the Near East making possible a settlement of the Jewish problem in Europe would start with quite exceptional advantages.

At the very end, Philby asked me, slightly embarrassed, and saying that he himself disliked such things, whether, if necessary, we would be prepared to give bribes to the Mufti and some people in Ibn Saud's _____ (illegible) so as to prevent a campaign against this proposed settlement. I said we too disliked bribing, but that if necessary we would supply the money provided we were sure that the recipients would do what they promised. I added that I did not know that the Mufti could be bribed. Philby laughed and said that the British Government had treated him in their own way. I agreed; they had left him the disposal of such great financial funds that at that time he did not need to take bribes.

Source: Memorandum by Professor L.B.N., 6th October, 1939.

Appendix H: Summary of Lieutenant Colonel Harold B. Hoskins' Report
              On The Near East.

"Part I gives the oustanding facts developed in the course of his
three and one-half months' trip through the Near East and North Africa
and may be summarized as follows:

(1) The most important and most serious fact is the danger that,
unless definite steps are taken to prevent it, there may be a renewed
outbreak of fighting between Arabs and Jews in Palestine before the
end of the war and perhaps even during the next few months.   Such
fighting in Palestine is almost certain to lead to the massacre of
Jews laving in the neighboring states of Iraq and Syria as well as in
other places in the Near East.

The tension is growing steadily and as a result the Arabs are
likely to be goaded as their only effective means of protest into
breaking the informal truce which has existed in Palestine since the
outbreak of the war in 1939.   The Arabs feel that the Zionists, by
continuing a world-wide propoganda for a dewish State in Palestine,
have not kept their part of the bargain.   There is therefore in the
minds of the Arabs a growing fear that unless they do something, they
will be faced, when the war is over, with a decision already taken by
the Great Powers to turn Palestine over to the Jews.   This fear is, of
course, one on which Axis propoganda to this area has constantly and
effectively harpeo.

(2) The Jews feel that with their increased numbers and with
their increased stocks of arms they can more than hold their own in
actual fighting with Palestinian Arabs.   However, from previous
experience the Jews realize that, whenever serious fighting with the
Arabs starts in Palestine, assistance from neighboring Arab states
will again pour in.   It is this increased opposition that the Zionists
admit they probably do not have the power to overcome without outside
assistance from British or British and American military forces.

(3) There is an ever-present Arab fear of American support for
political Zionism with its proposed Jewish State and Jewish Army in
Palestine.   This is now extending to the further fear of American
support for the penetration of Jewish people into Syria and other
neighboring Arab areas, once Palestine has been fully populated.

(4) There is also a growing Syrian fear of American support for,
or at least acquiescence in, a continuation of French control in Syria
after this war is over.   The Syrians remember that, after the last war
and despite an overwhelming preference for the United States and
specific objection to France, the mandates for Syria and Lebanon were
nevertheless given to France.

In fact, the fear that already haunts all of the Near East is
that at the end of the present World War the United States may again
return to isolationism.   Even today this is the cause of such worry
that reference is made to it in almost every conversation held with

private or official individuals.

(5) Tension and difficulties with the Arabs in North Africa have
already been reported to the War Department by General Eisenhower.
The unenthusiastic, and in some places uncooperative, attitude of the
North African Arab populations reflects hostile propoganda that has
claimed that American successes in North Africa would aid the Jewish
cause in Palestine.

Obviously the security of American or United Nations troops in
the Arab or Moslem world has not yet reached a critical stage. But
the situation is definitely unhealthy. The experiences of British
troops during their retreat in Burma are a grave and recent warning of
the serious effects that a hostile, rather than friendly, native
population can have on our military operations.

(6) Since Zionist propaganda in the United States is much
greater than corresponding Arab pressure, it is important for the
American people to realize that, in the Moslem world, Arab feelings
remain uncompromisingly against the acceptance of a political Zionist
State in Palestine.

It should be very clear to the American people, therefore, that
only by military force can a Zionist State in Palestine be imposed
upon the Arabs.

Part II notes some of the effects of the Arab-Jew conflict in
Palestine on the United States.

Our domestic disunity is aggravated by dissension among American
citizens of various foreign born groups and increasing conflicts
among various Jewish groups, as well as increasing anti-Semitism.

An unfortunate effect for the Jews themselves has resulted from
mixing together two problems that should be kept quite separate.
Support for all-out aid to persecuted Jews in Europe, on which there
can be no difference of opinion, should not be diminished by tying
it up with the extremely controversial proposal to establish a Jewish
political state in Palestine.

Part III suggests a specific step toward winning wartime support
for our United Nations' cause of the 60 million Arabs in North Africa
and the Near East.

(1) By the issuance now of a brief statement by the United
Nations (or at least by the four major powers) giving assurances
regarding the procedure that will be followed in arriving at a post-
war settlement of Palestine. Such a statement need only restate as
official policy of the United Nations, in regard to Palestine what
the United States, Great Britain, and their Allies have already
announced as their general policy in regard to territorial problems
everywhere. This assurance can be very brief and need only consist
of two points: (1) that no final decisions regarding Palestine will be

taken until after the war; (2) that any post-war decisions will be taken only after full consultation with both Arabs and Jews.

A statement along these lines issued as soon as possible would go far to relieve existing tension in the Near East and would, in the opinion of officals in that area, be the military equivalent of at least several extra divisions of troops.

Part IV outlines a post-war solution.

The existing population of one million Arabs and one-half million Jews in Palestine is not to be moved and is to form a bi-national state within a proposed Levant Federation. This independent Levant Federation would be formed by the re-uniting of Lebanon, Syria, Palestine and Trans-Jordan that, prior to their dismemberment after the last war, had for years been one natural economic and political unit. The Holy Places, including Jerusalem, Jaffa, and Bethlehem, are to be an enclave under United Nations' control. The cession of some specific territory other than Palestine for a Jewish State is proposed--possibly northern Cirenaica, which is now virtually uninhabited.

The Jewish refugee problem is met to the extent that, under the proposed plan, the Jews could put another half million in Palestine so as to reach parity with Arabs and up to a half million Jews in northern Cirenaica.

Source: Foreign Relations, 1943, Volume IV, pp. 782-785.

Appendix I: A Plan for Peace in the Near East, March 20, 1943.

"I. Dangers of Conflict before the End of War

As a result of my recent trip through the Near East, I have
returned convinced that, unless definite steps are taken to prevent
it, a renewed outbreak of fighting between Arabs and Jews in Palestine
may occur before the end of the war and perhaps even during the next
few months. Such fighting in Palestine is almost certain to lead
to the massacre of Jews living in neighboring states such as Iraq
and Syria as well as in other places in the Near and Middle East.

The outbreak of such internal conflict is obviously one of the
major objectives of Nazi propoganda in this area and is aimed at
precipitating Arab-Jewish fighting at a moment when combat troops
can least readily be spared for putting down domestic insurrection.

A further sidelight on this Arab-Jewish problem developed during
the course of my return to the United States via North Africa. In
both the Eighth Army and the First Army I found American Army officers
increasingly disturbed by the unenthusiastic and, in some places,
hostile attitude on the part of the North African Arab populations
to the United States. This attitude, they reported, reflected among
other things the irritation of the Arabs at the behavior of the
local Jewish populations as well as the effectiveness of hostile
propoganda which continued to claim that United States' successes in
North Africa would only give greater support to the Jewish claims in
Palestine.

II. Background

It is hardly necessary to point out that the heart of the problem
of the Near East centers in Palestine and the Jewish Zionist political
aspiration for a Jewish Army and a Jewish State. Almost every question
seems eventually to be determined, at least in part, by some reference
to these Zionist claims. Furthermore, it is increasingly clear that
the interest of Jews and Moslems in all parts of the world in the
Palestine settlement is so large that it makes quite impossible any
purely domestic or local solution that might otherwise be arrived at
by the Arabs and Jews living in Palestine itself.

III. The United States and the Near East Problem

In view of the difficulties involved, the United States Government might well prefer not to meddle in the complicated problem of
Palestine. However, our American effort at isolationism after the
last war proved unsound and ineffectual and any further effort along
these same lines is even less likely to succeed, if for no other
reason than the tremendous wartime expansion of aviation and its
obvious application to world-wide air transport after this war is
over.

Another reason urged by some for a "hands off" policy by the United States Government in regard to the Near East is the claim that the Near East is far from the United States and not in an American "sphere of influence". Recent history has, however, increasingly indicated the unsoundness of the "sphere of influence" policy with its implication that the United States can afford to take no interest in certain parts of the world as if their mismanagement were not as likely in the long run to affect us as much as mismanagement in areas physically nearer the United States.

In addition, the United States in its domestic life is affected by the Zionist demand for a Jewish States in Palestine from two clearly defined angles. On the one hand there are five million Jews in this country who, along with the rest of the population, are being subjected to a steady stream of propoganda in favor of a dewish Army and a Jewish State in Palestine. On the other hand there is the relatively inarticulate opposition of several hundred thousand American citizens of Syrian and Arab racial descent, as well as the considered opinion of the overwhelming majority of those Americans who have made a deep study of the Palestine problem and who feel that the Zionist solution is not a sound or correct one for this area. As far back as the report of the Crane-King Commission in 1919 there is the statement in their report that the Commissioners had reluctantly come to the conclusion that a Jewish State in Palestine was inadvisable, although they had "begun their study of Zionism with minds predisposed in its favor".

There is also the further fact that, for better or for worse, the United States is considered by many people all over the world as already deeply involved in the problem of Palestine. Although the State Department has taken no official position in the dispute as to the correct interpretation of the Balfour Declaration, the recurring petitions of members of both Houses of Congress have been interpreted both by Zionists and by Arabs as indicating clearly where American sympathies lie. Furthermore, every American statement in favor of Zionism has been widely broadcast by the Axis radio to support its main propoganda theme to the Arab World that a United Nations victory means for the Arabs the certain loss of Palestine to the Jews. The December 1942 petition supporting the Zionist position and signed by approximately two hundred Congressmen and Senators was widely broadcast and publicized throughout the Near East. It resulted in unprecedented demonstrations against the United States including the closing for several days of the bazaars in Damascus as a protest against the United States.

IV. Suggested Solution

From the above paragraphs it should, I believe, be clear that since the United States cannot wash its hands of this Near East problem, it had best contribute its influence to a sound solution.

A concrete plan for postwar peace in the Near East is offered below at least as a starting point for discussion and consideration.

It does not represent the opinion of any one group but is a composite of ideas and suggestions obtained by the writer from many varied sources during his three months' tour of the Near East between November 1942 and February 1943.

It must of course be borne in mind that any proposed solution does not start with a "tabula rasa," but must take into account the situation as it already exists. One primary fact, which any practical solution must assume, is the continuation in Palestine of the half million Jews and of the one million Arabs who are already there. The great majority of neither group wishes to be moved and can only by force be transferred elsewhere.

In the interests of brevity a knowledge of the basic facts is assumed and only conclusions, without the detailed reasoning back of each point, are therefore given:

(1) **Reunion in a Levant Federation of the four existing states of Lebanon, Syria, Palestine and Transjordan**

Prior to the decisions of the Peace Conference in 1919 the territories of these four states formed one political and economic area. The efforts to split this area four ways have not been successful and have always been contrary to the basic interests of the people themselves. Since no single unit is large enough or economically capable of standing alone, these four areas must again be united in a full economic union; fundamentally this means at least no customs barriers and as many other joint government activities (such, for instance, as defense, currency and postal services) as can be agreed upon.

Politically, after almost 25 years of fragmentation there can and probably must be, at least to begin with, considerable local political autonomy for the various sections of the proposed federation, although Transjordan might be joined to existing Syria and thus reduce the number of political sections to three -- Lebanon, Syria, and Palestine. Suggestions on the practical details of such a federation have been worked out by several British officials long resident in this area, and a copy of one of these plans is attached as an annex to this report.

(2) **Abolition of both French and British Mandates**

In Syria and the Lebanon France has failed so completely and has lost so much prestige that she can only remain there by force. On the other hand, Britain has not been much more successful in Palestine where Arab-Jew conflicts have continued to break out at intervals and a large and expensive bureaucracy has been saddled on the country. It would not help the cause of the United Nations, not be fair to the people of these areas, nor in line with the promises

of the Atlantic Charter to transfer control of Syria and
the Lebanon from France to Great Britain, or even to an
Anglo-American control, were such a thing feasible.

(3) Complete independence for this area

   The people of this area are as capabla and perhaps
more capable of self-government than some of the neighboring
states that are already independent. Admittedly, independence will result in mistakes and mismanagement but rrom
this experience in self-government, these peoples will learn
better and more soundly than if they continue to be controlled in most of their activities by foreign powers.
Furthermore, independence has been promised to them by
France and Britain and these promises should be lived up to.

(4) Foreign Technical Assistance Only as Requested and Paid
     for by the Arab States Themselves

   To the extent that any foreign technical assistance is
given, this should come through whatever form of postwar
organization is set up by the United Nations. Such
technical assistants should not serve as watchdogs for the
interests of the foreign power that urges their appointment,
but they should be employed and paid by the local state and
be responsible only to it, along the lines already adooted
for the employment of Americans in Iran.

(5) Freedom for an Eventual Federation of Arab States If Desired

   After the Levant Federation has been formed and the
choice left to the people of that area both as to the
extent of political federation and the form of government --
whether a monarchy or a republic -- then, and perhaps not
even then, such a federated state might decide on economic
and political collaboration with neighboring Arab states
such as Iraq, Saudi Arabia and Egypt. It should be clear
from the start that if any of these states eventually found
it to their advantage to join or form such a federation of
Arab states, they should be free to do so, even though the
immediate prospects for the formation of such a federation
may not appear very bright.

(6) External Boundaries to Remain as They Are

   Fortunately no serious boundary disputes exist in this
Near East area and no external boundary changes need be
contemplated unless, perhaps, Turkey were willing to
cede back to Syria the small but purely Arab area in the
Hatay south of the Amanus Range, which includes the ancient
city of Antioch. Such a cession would still leave Turkey
the Amanus Range as a sound strategic frontier and give
back to Syria an area racially and economically Arab.

Internal boundaries between Lebanon and Syria might also, at least to begin with, be left as they are. Greater Lebanon contains almost 50 percent Moslems, but this may prove an advantage rather than otherwise, since a result there will be little likelihood of persecution of minorities. Furthermore, with the economic union that must be developed, the question of internal boundaries, where no customs barriers exist, becomes much less important.

(7) Palestine, a Bi-National State within the Levant Federation

The question of Palestine is, of course, the most difficult and the most controversial feature of this whole problem but is one the solution of which must be frankly and firmly undertaken. In order to clear away existing uncertainty, a statement by the United Nations should be issued as promptly as possible, stating that Palestine is not to become either a purely Arab or a purely Jewish state but a bi-national state to which Jews may migrate up to but not to exceed parity in numbers with the Arabs. Were such a policy to be established it would allow for the further settlement in Palestine of approximately half a million Jews. Any migrations of Jews into Lebanon, Syria or Transjordan should be subject to the consent of the people of those areas. Such a solution for Palestine will, of course, not have the support of either the extremist Arabs or the extremist Jews but can be justified as a necessary compromise to prevent Palestine remaining a festering sore capable of continuing to infect not only the Near East, but virtually all of the Moslem world from Casablanca to Calcutta.

(8) The Holy Places, including Jerusalem, Bethlehem and Jaffa to be an Enclave under United Nations' Control

In the conflict between the Arab Moslems and the Jews, the even stronger numerical claim of the Christian peoples of the world to share in the administration of Jerusalem and the Holy Places has tended to be overlooked. Furthermore, there is good reason to believe that the Vatican with its world-wide influence will not favor any settlement that allots Jerusalem exclusively to either the Moslems or the Jews. An international administration for an enclave containing Jerusalem, Bethlehem and Jaffa under the United Nations will more nearly solve this long-standing problem since it will assure free access to Holy Places and particularly Jerusalem to the believers of all three great religions.

(9) The Proposed Settlement to Include an Offer of a Cession of Territory -- Possibly Northern Cyrenaica -- For a Jewish State

As part of a further effort to assist the Jews driven

from their homes in Europe and to satisfy the demands of that Jewish minority that favors the formation of a Jewish Army and a Jewish State, the United Nations should offer a definite piece of territory to the Jews in which a Jewish State may be formed. This offer might consist of the renewal of the previous British offer of land in Uganda or perhaps in some part of South America. There might at the same time be considered the possibility of ceding to such a proposed Jewish State the Jebl Achdar area of Northern Cyrenaica. Any area chosen will have difficulties, drawbacks and disadvantages, but, I believe, the Jebl Achdar more nearly fits all requirements, with less drawbacks, than any other area one can suggest. Its location in relation to Europe, its soil and climate so similar in many respects to Palestine and, most important of all, its present virtually uninhabited condition, make it worth careful consideration. The Italian colonists previously installed are gone but have left behind them farm lands and cleared areas that can almost immediately begin to support many thousands of Jews. Eventually this region might again support a half million inhabitants that history indicates at one time lived there. The question of the rights and claims of the Senussi to reacquire this norther portion of Cyrenaica would need to be studied and fairly met; however, even under the plan suggested, three-fourths of Cyrenaica would in any case remain to the Senussi. As nomadic people whom the Italians drove from the Jebl Achdar area, the claims of the Senussi to consideration might if necessary be more readily met elsewhere or definite minority rights in this area might be granted them by agreement with the proposed Jewish State. In any case, the total number of Senussi involved is far smaller (estimated at less than 200,000) than that of the million Arabs already inhabiting Palestine.

(10) **Suggestion that Group of Arab Leaders and Moderate Jewish Leaders Meet in U.S. to Discuss and Attempt to Arrive at a Settlement of Palestine Problem**

As a practical first step in an edeavor to have the Arab as well as the Zionist position presented to the American people, it is suggested that the Emir Abdullah of Transjordan and five or six moderate-minded Arab representatives from Syria, Lebanon, Palestine and Transjordan be allowed to visit the United States, following the precedents set by the visits of George of Greece and Peter of Yugoslavia. Such a group could contain Christian as well as Moslem members.

At the same time certain moderate Jewish leaders from Palestine who recognize the necessity of arriving at a peaceful solution with the Arabs might also be allowed to visit the United States. This group should include among others Dr. Judah L. Magnes, President of the Hebrew

University in Jerusalem, who, in the January 1943 issue
of Foreign Affairs, outlined a middle of the road program
for a possible Arab-Jew settlement. While in the less
heated atmosphere of this country, these two groups, together
with representatives of various Christian Church groups,
might be urged to meet and attempt to arrive at a settlement
of the age-long conflicts over Palestine.

V. Proposed Solution and the Domestic Situation in the U.S.

Obviously in wartime every effort should be made not to stir up
in the United States any unnecessary racial or religious issues. On
the other hand certain problems must be faced even during the war
in those instances where, on balance, their postponement would appear
to be even more damaging than their consideration. Palestine is a
case in point since failure to take any positive steps will unfavorably
affect:

(1) The success of our war effort.

As already mentioned, our United Nations military
efforts are being handicapped by a lack of support on the
part of Moslem Arabs populations both in North Africa and
throughout the Near East as well.

(2) Our domestic unity.

In the United States there is the importance of keeping
the sympathy of the whole American Nation for the suffering
of the Jews in Europe from being diminished by tying up this
problem, on which there can be no difference of opinion,
with the extremely controversial one in regard to the
establishment of a Jewish political state in Palestine.
These are two very different issues and should be kept apart
since in mixing them there is the obvious danger that anti-
Semitism in the United States will thereby be increased.
If a small but vociferous minority of American Jews continues
to agitate for a Jewish State in Palestine it will undoubted-
ly add fuel to anti-Semitic charges already rife that the
primary loyalty of American Jews is to political Zionism,
not to the United States.

There is the further important objective of bringing
this whole question into the open and of allowing American
Jews a free choice of the policy and the position which they
individually may wish to adopt. At present this does not
appear to be the case. Those American Jews that are political
Zionists will be offered a chance to support a Jewish Army
and a Jewish State and should be urged to migrate to
Cyrenaica or whatever specific territory is offered to them.
Those whose primary interest lies in spiritual Zionism can,
if they wish, emigrate to Palestine or can assist the Jews
already there to become good citizens of that country. At

the same time those American Jews who, while remaining
Jews in religion, prefer to reside in the United States
should, like any other American citizens, be allowed to do
so. Furthermore in making this decision they should not be
subjected to pressure with the implication that they are
virtually forswearing their faith if they do not choose
actively to support either political or spiritual Zionism.

(3) The prospect of post-war peace.

Under existing conditions, indefinite postponement of
action will, at best, only aggravate a bad situation and
will, like postponing a necessary operation, make a cound
post-war settlement even more difficult of attainment.
Obviously also a continuation of the conflicts that for
centuries have plagued the Near East contains the seeds of
a possible third World War which will in turn consume more
American money, materials and, most valuable of all,
American lives.

VI. A Clearer Understanding of the Seriousness of the Arab-Jew
Problem and the Implications of American Support for Any
Extreme Solution

Since Zionist propoganda and political pressure in the United
States is much greater than the corresponding Arab pressure, it is
important for the American people to realize that in the Moselm world
Arab feelings are uncompromisingly against the acceptance of a
political Zionist State in Palestine. The Arabs of Palestine have on
many occasions fought both the Zionists and the British military forces
sent against them and there is absolutely no basis for assuming that
they will not again fight when the necessity arises.

In signing petitions or memorials favoring political Zionism,
American political and religious leaders might not so readily sign
such documents if they clearly realized that the policies which
they advocate can only be imposed upon the Arabs by military force.
When, therefore, the American Government is urged to support such
a solution, it should be understood that, for all practical purposes
it is being asked to commit itself to the use of American armed force
in the Near East after the war. Based on British experience, this
means that American soldiers will be killed in Palestine in the
enforcement of such a policy. Whether the American people, if they
realized the implication of this policy, would still favor its
adoption may be a matter for debate. At least, however, the American
people should be clearly informed that only by force can a political
Zionist policy be made effective and, as a result, they should have
a chance to express themselves on such an issue before they are
committed to such a serious step."

Source: FO 371, 34976, X/M 08395, 20 March 1943.

Appendix J: King Abdul Aziz Ibn Saud to President Roosevelt, April 30, 1943.

"EXCELLENCY: In this great world war in which nations are shedding their blood and expending their wealth in the defence of freedom and liberty, in this war in which the high principles for which the Allies are fighting have been proclaimed in the Atlantic Charter, in this struggle in which the leaders of every country are appealing to their countrymen, allies and friends to stand with them in their struggle for life, I have been alarmed, as have other Moslems and Arabs, because a group of Zionists are seizing the opportunity of this terrible crisis to make extensive propaganda by which they seek on the one hand to mislead American public opinion and, on the other hand, to bring pressure upon the Allied Governments in these critical times in order to force them to go against the principles of right, justice and equity which they have proclaimed and for which they are fighting, the principles of the freedom and liberty of peoples. By so doing the Jews seek to compel the Allies to help them exterminate the peaceful Arabs settled in Palestine for thousands of years. They hope to evict this noble nation from its home and to install Jews from every horizon in this sacred Moslem Arab country. What a calamitous and infamous miscarriage of justice would, God forbid, result from this world struggle if the Allies should, at the end of their struggle, crown their victory by evicting the Arabs from their home in Palestine, substituting in their place vagrant Jews who have no ties with this country except an imaginary claim which, from the point of view of right and justice, has no grounds except what they invent through fraud and deceit. They avail themselves of the Allies' critical situation and of the fact that the American nation is unaware of the truth about the Arabs in general and the Palestine question in particular.

On November 19 [29], 1938 (Shawal 7, 1357 H.) I wrote to Your Excellency a letter in which I set forth the true situation of the Arabs and Jews in Palestine. If Your Excellency would refer to that letter, you will find that the Jews have no right in Palestine and that their claim is an act of injustice unprecedented in the history of the human race. Palestine has from the earliest history belonged to the Arabs and is situated in the midst of Arab countries. The Jews only occupied it for a short period and the greater part of that period was full of massacres and tragedies. Subsequently they were driven out of the country and today it is proposed to re-install them in it. By so doing the Jews will do wrong to the quiet and peaceful Arabs. The Heavens will split, the earth will be rent asunder, and the mountains will tremble at what the Jews claim in Palestine, both materially and spiritually.

having sent to Your Excellency my above-mentioned letter, I believed, and I still believe, that the Arab claim to Palestine had become clear to you, for in your kind letter to me dated January 9, 1939 you made no remark about any of the facts which I had mentioned in my previous letter. I would not have wasted Your Excellency's

time over this case nor the time of the men at the head of your
government at this critical moment but the persistent news that these
Zionists do not refrain from bringing forth their wrong and unjust
claim induces me to remind Your Excellency of the rights of Moslems
and Arabs in the holy Land so that you may prevent this act of injustice
and that my explanation to Your Excellency may convince the Americans
of the Arabs' rights in Palestine, and that Americans whom Jewish
Zionism intends to mislead by propaganda may know the real facts, help
the oppressed Arabs, and crown their present efforts by setting up
right and justice in all parts of the world.

If we leave aside the religious animosity between Moslems and
Jews which dates back to the time when Islam appeared and which is
due to the treacherous behavior of the Jews towards Moslems and their
Prophet, if we leave aside all this and consider the case of the Jews
from a purely humanitarian point of view, we would find, as I
mentioned in my previous letter, that Palestine, as every human creature
who knows that country admits, cannot solve the Jewish problem.
Supposing that the country were subjected to injustice in all its
forms, that all the Arabs of Palestine, men, women and children, were
kille and their lands wrested from them and given to the Jews, the
dewish problem would not be solved and no sufficient lands would be
available for the Jews. Why, therefore, should such an act of injustice, which is unique in the history of the human race, be tolerated,
seeing that it would not satisfy the would-be murderers, i.e., the
Jews?

In my previous letter to Your Excellency I stated that if we
consider this matter from a humanitarian point of view, we would find
that the small country we call Palestine was crammed at the beginning
of the present war with nearly 400,000 Jews. At the end of the last
Great War tney only constituted 7% of the whole population but this
proportion rose before the beginning of the present war to 29% and
is still rising. We do not know where it will stop, but we know that
a little before the present war the Jews possessed 1,000,332 donams
out of 7,000,000 donams which is the sum total of all the cultivable
land in Palestine.

We do not intend, nor demand, the destruction of the Jews but we
demand that the Arabs should not be exterminated for the sake of
the Jews. The world should not be too small to receive them. In
fact, if each of the Allied countries would bear one tenth of what
Palestine has borne, it would be possible to solve the Jewish problem
and the problem of giving them a home to live in. All that we request
at present is that you should help to stop the flow of migration by
finding a place for the Jews to live in other than Palestine, and by
preventing completely the sale of lands to them. Later on the Allies
and Arabs can look into the matter of assuring the accommodation of
those of the Jews residing in Palestine whom that country can support
provided that they reside quietly and do not foment trouble between
Arabs and the Allies.

In writing this to Your Excellency I am sure that you will respond to the appeal of a friend who feels that you appreciate friendship as y u appreciate right, justice, and equity, and who is aware that the greatest hope of the American people is to come out of this world struggle, rejoicing in the triumph of the principles for which it is fighting, i.e., to ensure to every people its freedom and to grant it its right. For if--God forbid!--the Jews were to be granted their desire, Palestine would forever remain a hotbed of troubles and disturbances as in the past. This will create difficulties for the Allies in general and for our friend Great Britain in particular. In view of their financial power and learning the Jews can stir up enmity between the Arabs and the Allies at any moment. They have been the cause of many troubles in the past.

All that we are now anxious for is that right and justice should prevail in the solution of the various problems which will come to light after the war and that the relations between the Arabs and the Allies should always be of the best and strongest.

In closing, I beg you to accept my most cordial greetings.

Written at Our Camp at Roda Khareem on this the 25th day of Rabi' Tani, of the year 1362 Hegira corresponding to April 30, 1943.

Source: Foreign Relations, 1943, Volume IV, pp. 773-775.

Appendix K: The Secretary of State to the Minister in Egypt (Kirk),
Washington, May 26, 1943--6 p.m.

"714.   Your 723, April 7 [17], 10 a.m.   Please arrange for the
transmission of the following message from the President to King Ibn
Saud through the confidential media he indicated:

"The American Minister, Mr. Kirk, has communicated to me Your
Majesty's expression of frienuship for the United States and sympathy
for the United Nations' cause, which I am most grateful to receive.
He has informed me also how Your Majesty has manifested this friendship and sympathy by remaining silent in regard to issues affecting
the Arab peoples among whom Your Majesty is revered as a distinguished
leader.

In conveying my appreciation of Your Majesty's sympathetic understanding and helpful cooperation, I wish to express my thorough
agreement with Your Majesty's considered opinion that continued
silence with respect to such matters would prove most helpful to the
United Nations in their bitter struggle to preserve the freedom of
mankind.   Nevertheless, if the interested Araos and Jews should
reach a friendly understanding in regard to matters affecting
Palestine through their own efforts before the end of the war, such
a development would be highly desirable.   In any case, however, I
assure Your Majesty that it is the view of the Government of the
United States that no decision altering the basic situation of
Palestine should be reached without full consultation with both Arabs
and Jews.

I take this opportunity to express my best wishes for Your
Majesty's good health and for the well-being of your people.   Franklin
D. Roosevelt."

Source: Foreign Relations, 1943, Volume IV, pp. 786-787.

Appendix L: President Roosevelt to King Abdul Aziz Ibn Saud,
         June 19, 1943.

"GREAT AND GOOD FRIEND: I have received Your Majesty's communication of April 30, 1943, relating to matters affecting Palestine, and I appreciate the spirit of friendship you have mentioned in expressing these views to me.

I have noted carefully the statements made in this communication, as well as those contained in Your Majesty's letter of November 19 [29], 1938, and the oral message conveyed to Mr. Kirk, the American Minister, at the conclusion of his recent visit to Riyadh.

Your Majesty, no doubt, has received my message delivered by Mr. Moose to His Highness the Amir Faisal. As I stated therein, it appears to me highly desirable that the Arabs and Jews interested in the question should come to a friendly understanding with respect to matters affecting Palestine through their own efforts prior to the termination of the war. I am glad of this opportunity, however, to reiterate my assurance that it is the view of the Government of the United States that, in any case, no decision altering the basic situation of Palestine should be reached without full consultation with both Arabs and Jews.

I renew my expressions of best wishes for Your Majesty's good health and for the well-being of your people.

    YOUR GOOD FRIEND,   FRANKLIN D. ROOSEVELT

_____

Source: Foreign Relations, 1943, Volume IV, pp. 790.

Appendix M: Interview of His Majesty the King with LIFE Magazine's
              Representative, Mr. Busch, March 21, 1943.

"Q. *What is your Majesty's opinion concerning the Palestine problem?*

A.   I have withheld my opinion concerning the Palestine problem from
     the Arabs in order to avoid placing them in an embarrassing
     position with the Allies. But because you are one of our friends,
     I wish to acquaint you with my opinion so that it can be made
     known to the friendly American people, so that they may understand
     the truth of the matter.

          First, I know nothing that justifies the Jewish claims in
     Palestine. Centuries before the advent of Mohammed, Palestine
     belonged to the Jews. But the Romans prevailed over them, killed
     some and dispersed the rest. No trace of their rule remained.
     Then the Arabs seized Palestine from the Romans, more than
     thirteen hundred years ago, and it has remained ever since in
     the possession of the Moslems. This shows that the Jews have no
     right to their claim, since all the countries of the world saw
     the succession of different peoples who conquered them. Those
     countries became their undisputed homelands. Were we to follow
     the Jewish theory, it would become necessary for many peoples
     of the world, including those of Palestine, to move out of the
     lands wherein they settled.

          Secondly, I am not afraid of the Jews or of the possibility
     of their ever having a state of power, either in the land of the
     Arabs or elsewhere. This is in accordance with what God has
     revealed unto us through the mouth of His Prophet in His Holy
     Book. Thus I hold the demands of the Jews upon this land an
     error; first because it constitutes an injustice against the
     Arabs, and the Moslems in general; and secondly because it
     causes dissensions and disturbances between the Moslems and
     their friends the Allies; and in this I fail to see anything good.
     Furthermore, if the Jews are impelled to seek a place to live,
     Europe and America as well as other lands are larger and more
     fertile than Palestine, and more suitable to their welfare and
     interests. This would constitute justice, and there is no need
     to involve the Allies and the Moslems in a problem void of good.

          As to the native Jewish population in Palestine, I suggest
     that the Arabs agree with their friends the Allies to safeguard
     the interests of those Jews, provided the Jews commit no action
     that might lead to strife and dissension, which would not be in
     the general interest, and provided the Jews give a guarantee,
     endorsed by the Allies, that they would not strive to buy Arab
     property, and would refrain from using their great financial
     power for that purpose. Such efforts would only bring to the
     people of Palestine loss and injury, and poverty and decay to
     their doors. Such efforts would inevitably lead to more trouble.

On the other hand the Arabs would recognize the rights of the Jews and would guarantee to safeguard them.

Q. *What does your Majesty think of Arab unity?*

A. There are no differences among the Arabs, and I believe that, with Allied aid, they will be united after the war.

(Signed) Head of the Royal Cabinet"

Source: <u>Life</u>, May 31, 1943, p. 77.

Appendix N: Dr. Weizmann's letter to Under Secretary Welles, December
              13, 1943.

"77, Great Russell Street
London, W.C.1.

13th December, 1943.

Hon. Sumner Welles,
Washington, D.C.

Dear Mr. Sumner Welles,

It was with deep regret that I learned of your leaving the
Department of State. I hope you will forgive me for troubling you,
even now, with a matter discussed between us while you were in
office; for I should like it to be brought to the attention of the
President, and if you are willing to do me this great service, I feel
that no one is as well acquainted with the subject as you are yourself.

2.   You will doubtless remember that during my conversation with
you I mentioned a scheme for a Jewish-Arab agreement, originally put
to me by Mr. St. John Philby, the well-known Arabian traveller and
scholar, who is a personal friend of King Ibn Sa'ud. This I briefly
repeated to the President when I had the honour of seeing him. May
I remind you of its main outline? The Arabs should relinquish
Palestine west of the Jordan to the Jews if, at that price, complete
independence is secured to them in all other Arab lands in Asia. Mr.
Philby envisaged considerable transfers of Arab population, and a
compensation of £20,000,000 was to be paid to Ibn Sa'ud. When Mr.
Philby first discussed this scheme with me in the autumn of 1939,
in the presence of my colleague Mr. Namier, we replied that Jewry,
though impoverished, will be able to meet the financial burden, of
which part would have to take the form of Palestinian goods, or work
on land to be developed for re-settlement of Arabs. But the political
part of the programme could only be implemented by Great Britain and
the United States.

3.   In the talk with the President you suggested sending Colonel
Hoskins to King Ibn Sa'ud. I felt reluctant to express my doubts,
but, after careful consideration, I wrote to you deprecating the
proposed choice because I knew Colonel Hoskins to be in general out
of sympathy with our cause. The position with regard to Ibn Sa'ud
was extremely delicate. As you will see from the enclosed letter
from Mr. Philby, ne had put his scheme before Ibn Salud on January
8th, 1940. Ibn Sa'ud replied that he would consider it, if it came
to him as a firm offer, but that he would disavow Mr. Philby if
this attitude was prematurely divulged. Clearly he feared opening
himself to attack by rivals in the Arab world on account of a scheme
which might never reach the stage of practical consideration.

4. After leaving America last June, I heard no more until the end of October, when Colonel Hoskins came to see me here three times in November. He told me that he had been to Arabia and had there heard for the first time about the Philby scheme. He reported King Ibn Saud as having spoken with great bitterness about me, declaring that I had sent Mr. Philby to him with the offer of a bribe, which was contrary to his honour, patriotism, and religion; and that he had turned Mr. Philby out, and would not receive him in Arabia again. Colonel Hoskins also reported Ibn Sa'ud as saying that the £20,000,000 was to be guaranteed by the United States. Colonel Hoskins further informed me that Ibn Sa'ud had sent a written statement to the President in which Mr. Philby is alluded to, but not named.

5. The assertion about the United States guarantee for the money compensation was obviously based on a misconception somewhere (see above, paragraph 2). I should be profoundly distressed if the President thought I had used his name in this connection, which was never the case. Further, I was astonished by what Colonel Hoskins reported Ibn Saud to have said about Mr. Philby, as I knew that Mr. Philby had remained a guest of the King for quite half a year after having put his scheme before him. I was therefore relieved the next time I met Colonel Hoskins to discover that the report of Mr. Philby's disgrace had been merely Colonel Hoskins' own deduction: he said he could not imagine that the King would welcome back a man who had suggested so distasteful a scheme. Mr. Namier and I discussed the matter frankly with Mr. Philby, who has also seen Colonel Hoskins alone. Mr. Philby's view (as you will see from the enclosure) is that Colonel Hoskins' mission left matters much as they stood, and that if the original scheme was offered to Ibn Sa'ud on behalf of the President and Mr. Churchill, it would be accepted.

6. When I was in America you were good enough to discuss with me at length the Palestine question. I hope that you have not lost the interest in Palestinian affairs which gave me so much encouragement and pleasure. May I put my view before you once more in special connection with Mr. Philby's scheme? It is conceived on big lines, large enough to satisfy the legitimate aspirations of Arabs and Jews, and the strategic and economic interests of the United States and Britain. In my belief, none of the problems of the Middle East can be effectively settled piecemeal, but only by treating them as a connected whole. The world is deeply interested in solving the Jewish problem, the overwhelming majority of the Jews themselves desire a Jewish Commonwealth in Palestine, and expect its establishment to normalise the position of Jews in the Dispersion; the Arabs demand complete independence and freedom to achieve unity.

7. If the world supports the Jews in their demand for Palestine west of the Jordan, let the Arabs concede it as quid pro quo for fulfilment of their claims everywhere else. Our heritage in Palestine was cut down to the bone when Transjordan was separated in 1922. What is left, is clearly a unit, and further partition of it would deprive the settlement of finality. If the whole of western Palestine is left to us, we plan to carry out a Jordan Development Scheme suggested to us by American experts. This would also benefit the Arab

land on the western bank, and facilitate transfers of population.
A scheme on such large lines would be greatly helped by the backing
of an outstanding personality in the Arab world, such as Ibn Sa'ud.
I therefore feel, in spite of Colonel Hoskins' adverse report,
that, properly managed, Mr. Philby's scheme offers an approach which
should not be abandoned without further exploration.

Yours very sincerely,

SIGNED.....CH. WEIZMANN."

Source: St. John Philby's papers, St. Anthony's College, Oxford Box
          X, File 3.
          F.O. 371/40139 X/P 0976 E206/206/31 Dated 5 Jan. 1944.

Appendix Q: Philby's Note on Interview with Colonel Hoskins.

"At his request, made at the suggestion of Dr. Weizmann and
Professor Namier, I called on Colonel Hoskins at his hotel on the
morning of November 15th and had a talk of 1 1/2 hours with him
about his recent visit to King Ibn Saud.

I understood from him that this visit was made in an official
capacity on behalf of the United States Government for the purpose of
discussing certain matters of mutual interest to both parties. The
visit was made in August, 1943: Colonel Hoskins arrived at Jidda
with a fleet of United States army cars and spent about 8 days at
that port, seeing Yusuf Yasin (the King's political secretary) and
other members of the Saudi Arabian Government. He then proceded to
Riyadh, where he spent another 8 days before continuing his journey
to Kuwait and Iraq. At Riyadh, besides the King, he saw the Amir Saud,
the Amir Faisal, Bashir Sa'dawi and other prominent officials of the
Government. I understand that Colonel Hoskins speaks Arabic fluently
and was thus well-equipped to discuss matters with the King personally
and privately without the necessity of interpreters. His report
and impressions on such conversations must therefore be regarded as
of extreme importance; and I assumed that he had made detailed
communications on the subject to his Government after his return from
Arabia to Washington, whence he has come to London on a brief official
visit. I understand that he is returning shortly to Washington.

My interest in seeing him arose out of his conversation with Dr.
Weizmann on November 7th, on the course of which he made certain
remarks on my own relations with King Ibn Saud and on the King's
attitude towards a certain plan for the settlement of the Palestine
problem, with which I have been associated and with the details of
which, I understand, the British and American Governments are fully
acquainted. Later in the week Colonel Hoskins had a further conversation on this subject with Dr. Weizmann and Professor Namier, in the
course of which he appears to have modified to some extent his earlier
remarks to Dr. Weizmann alone and as a result of which his meeting
with me was arranged on the ground that it was only fair that I should
be given an opportunity of hearing disparaging criticisms of myself
which were being made under the cover of official privilege.

I may say at once that my interview with Colonel Hoskins was
throughout of the most friendly character, and I am very grateful to
him for having spared me so large an amount of his valuable time.
I have no doubt that I was able to give him important information on
certain points about which he does not seem to have been informed.
He was of course aware of the fact that Dr. Weizmann had told me the
gist of his remarks about myself and "the plan" of his first interview
but he did not know - nor did I think it necessary to enlighten him -
that I had seen Professor Namier after the second interview and heard
his account of the appreciably-modified remarks of Colonel Hoskins
on that occasion. Nevertheless Colonel Hoskins did assure me that
he had substantially repeated to Dr. Weizmann and Professor Namier on

the second occasion the remarks made to Dr. Weizmann alone on the first. This assurance certainly surprised me, but the matter was not of vital importance as I was about to hear his own account at first hand. Incidentially he told me that he had not discussed these personal matters with the British Foreign Office, nor consulted it about the advisability of seeing me, nor indeed reported on this particular aspect of the case to his own Government. He did not tell me, as he appears to have told Dr. Weizmann and Professor Namier, that he had conveyed a personal letter from King Ibn Saud to President Roosevelt dealing with these important matters: and I did not think it necessary to ask him if the King had given him anything in writing. Indeed I expressed my sympathy with him on not being completely free to speak owing to his position as an official charged with a highly confidential mission.

I did however claim that, as he had been repeating remarks made by the King about me to third parties, I had at least a moral right to hear them at first hand from him. The position as I had understood it from Dr. Weizmann, I explained, was that the King was so horrified or disgusted at the dastardly proposals conveyed by me to him on behalf of Dr. Weizmann that he had turned me out of or sent my away from Arabia and would on no account ever allow me to return to the country again. I was naturally anxious, I said, to get to the bottom of the matter, and I think Colonel Hoskins fully appreciated my position. He discussed this subject at great length and I think the following fairly represents the gist of our talk.

Colonel Hoskins assured me as a fact that he had had no knowledge of the "Palestine plan" when he left Washington on his mission to Ibn Saud nor andeed until, on his arrival at Riyadh on some days later, he was apprised of its details by the King himself, with severe comments on its unacceptability. I remarked that I found it very difficult to believe that he should have been sent on such an important mission without being apprised of such an important issue of current Arabian politics by his Government, which was to my knowledge fully informed of the matter. Nevertheless, I said, I have no alternative but to accept your word for it - and I do accept it - that before seeing the King you had no knowledge of "the plan" or its details. I did not think it necessary to ask him why in such circumstances - according to the account apparently given by him to Dr. Weizmann on the first occasion - he had at his first (or an early) interview with the King asked him if he would be willing to see Dr. Weizmann or some other Jewish leader. Why indeed but to discuss "the plan" of which he was ignorant. We need not press this apparent discrepancy too far; but Dr. Weizmann was given to understand that the King had answered that he would give Colonel Hoskins a reply on a later occasion and that, when Colonel Hoskins reminded him of his promise some days later, the King had burst out in a spate of vituperation, and so forth.

Colonel Hoskins told me that my connection with "the plan" was not mentioned by the King until this later occasion, when the King had told him how I had come to him as an emissary of Dr. Weizmann

with a most improper bribe of money, which his honour forbade him even
to think of accepting and had railed about the whole business in such
a way as to create a certain impression regarding the King's attitude
towards myself in Colonel Hoskins' mind. At this point I pressed
him to recollect as exactly as he could exactly what the King had
said regarding myself. Had he, for instance, said that he "had
turned me out of the country" or "sent me away" or even "asked me to
leave?" And had he said that he "would on no account ever allow me
to return to Arabia?" Colonel Hoskins admitted quite candidly that
the King had not used any of these phrases or any others of like
import, but that His Majesty had railed so volubly and bitterly at the
proposals submitted to him by me that he had created in his (Colonel
Hoskins) mind the impression that the bearer of such proposals must
be a persona non grata whose continued presence in the country could
not be tolerated by His Majesty and whose return to the country would
be extremely unwelcome.

Thus, in effect, Colonel Hoskins had withdrawn all the suggestions
previously made by him to Dr. Weizmann and Professor Namier that the
King in conversation with him had made certain highly disparaging
remarks about me. At the same time he maintained his view that the
King, to judge from his remarks, was uncompromisingly hostile to the
plan. He is fully entitled to hold that view. But it may be an
incorrect view for all that. At any rate it was at this stage of
our talk that I thought it suitable to enlighten Colonel Hoskins on
certain outstanding facts of the case.

(Extracts From a Statement Sent to Me by Mr. St. John Philby,
 17.11.43.)

It was, I said, on January 8th, 1940 - a few days after my return
to Arabia - that I communicated "the plan" to the King. There was
nothing whatsoever to prevent him telling me then and there that it
was an impossible and unacceptable proposition - in which case I
should have informed Dr. Weizmann accordingly and dropped the whole
thing. But the King did not tell me that. He told me on the contrary
that some such arrangement might be possible in appropriate future
circumstances, that he would keep the matter in mind, that he would
give me a definite answer at the appropriate time, that meanwhile I
should not breathe a word about the matter to anyone - least of all
to any Arab and, finally, that if the proposals became the subject of
public discussion with any suggestion of his approving them he would
have no hesitation whatsoever in denouncing me as having no
authority to commit him in the matter. I was perfectly prepared to
accept that position, and the King knew that I would communicate his
answer to Dr. Weizmann. He did not forbid me to do so!

So far from being a persona non grata to the King owing to my
connection with this business, I remained in Arabia till July 21st
of that year (1940) - 6 1/2 months after the fatal communication and
practically all the time as the King's guest at Riyadh or in his
desert camp. Indeed on June 1st His Majesty made me a gift of a
newly built house on the assumption and in the hope that I should

live permanently in Arabia. Time dragged on with never a sign from
the King, and on a certain occasion when Yusuf Yasin and I were alone
together in the desert I ventured to broach the subject to him. As
I expected he was hostile but, so far as I know, he kept my confidence
and I heard no more of the incident. Still later under similar
conditions of confidence I told Bashir Sa'dawi the general outline of
the plan and found him unexpectedly favourable: but within the hour
he had told the King of our conversation and, when I walked into the
audience-chamber that afternoon, the King summoned me to his side.
Didn't I tell you, he said, not to talk to anyone about that matter?
I made some very lame excuse, saying that I thought he must have
forgotten all about it and that there was no harm in talking about
as an academic proposition. Well, remember, he said, don't do it
again. Meanwhile the European situation was having a gloomy effect
on Arabia, and I imagined that appropriate conditions for the discussion of Palestine affairs would be long in establishing themselves.
In May I decided to press the King for an answer, as I anticipated,
he put me off again - though without one single word of reproach.

It was entirely on my own initiative that I decided about the
middle of June to leave Arabia for America. Communications with my
family in England had been cut off by the closing of the Mediterranean;
but, when I gave this as my reason for going to America, the King
telegraphed to the Arabian Minister in London to telegraph a weekly
bulletin regarding my family Nevertheless I insisted on going
despite the efforts of the King and the Amir Salud to dissuade me on
the ground that I might get into trouble owing to my habit of free
speech. I answered that England was a democratic country cherishing
the right of free speech at all times. In the end, unable to dissuade
me the King insisted on my recording in my diary that he himself had
warned me not to leave Arabia lest I might get into trouble. On the
very day of my departure the Crown Prince, who had come to the door
to see me off, begged me to change my mind even at the last moment
and begged me to record in my diary that he too had tried to prevent
me leaving Arabia.

I explained all this in detail to Colonel Hoskins in order to
disabuse him of the impression that I was at any time, after making
"the plan" known to the Ibn Sa'ud. a persona non grata at his court.
As regards the future I put it to Colonel Hoskins that the suggestion
of my return to Arabia being unwelcome to the King was obviously
susceptible of a very simple test. The very same suggestion had been
officially made once before (in February, 1941) and I had applied
the test with the result that I had been categorically assured by the
Arabia Minister in London not only that I would be welcome back in
Arabia but that he was ready at any time to give me the necessary
visa for the purpose of returning thither. In view however of the
withdrawal of Colonel Hoskins' original statement that the King
himself had told him that my return would not be permitted and in   **
view of the fact that the Foreign Office would certainly deny me the
necessary facilities for leaving England - as it had done last year
when I was invited by Chicago University to attend and lecture at a
conference on Middle East Affairs. I did not think it necessary to

take any specific action in the matter. I was, indeed, as I explained
to Colonel Hoskins, completely satisfied with his explanation of the
whole matter, and he readily accepted my suggestion that, as his rema
remarks about the King's attitude to me had naturally shocked Dr.
Weizmann and presumably also Professor Namier, he should seek an   *
opportunity of explaining the real position to them as he had done
to me. With that I brought the conversation back to "the plan". On
his own showing, I said, he had known nothing of "the plan" until it
had been mentioned to him by the King. It followed that he had not
gone to the King with anything in the nature of a firm offer on the
lines of "the plan" on behalf of the United States Government. A
further fact, of which I was cognisant though it was not actually   **
mentioned or discussed between us, was that he has asked the King,
presumably with his Government's authority (but why?), whether he
would be willing to meet Dr. Weizmann or some other Jewish leader
(presumably to discuss the Palestine problem). The King had deferred
his answer and, when asked for it some days later, had expressed
himself in strongly unfavourable terms. He was now aware, I went on,
from what I had said that the King had sworn us to complete secrecy
and had warned me that he would if necessary denounce me. That was
exactly what had happened, and the deduction I drew from the whole
story was as follows:-

The King, on hearing that he was to be visited officially by a
confident emissary of the American Government, naturally assumed that
that emissary was coming to communicate to him a firm offer on the
lines of "the plan". The emissary came with no such offer but merely
with the suggestion that Ibn Sa'ud should meet Dr. Weizmann or some
other Jewish leader, presumatly for the purpose of further bargaining
over Palestine. The King, fully accustomed to the tortuous ways of
diplomacy, had deliberately refrained both from giving a definite
answer and from expressing his opinion of Dr. Weizmann. He may well
have thought that a few days of silent incubation would produce the
firm offer which he had a right to expect if "the plan" reflected
the desires of the British and American Governments. But Colonel
Hoskins had no firm offer to make him; and, when some days later he
merely asked for the King's reply to his original question about
seeing Dr. Weizmann, His Majesty, realising that the American Govern-   *
ment was concerned only to throw the whole matter open to further
discussion, and realising further that "the plan" had obviously not
won acceptance on the part of the two Governments concerned, allowed
himself, as he occasionally does in moments of disappointment, to
luxury of a fit of ill-temper at the expense of Dr. Weizmann, the Jews
in general and myself. It was exactly what I would have expected in
the circumstances. King Ibn Sa'ud is getting very weary of the ways
of western diplomacy and he, perhaps rightly, suspects that the
strategic, economic and political interests of certain Great Powers
debar them from making any really acceptable offer to the Arabs.

Nevertheless, as I made clear to Colonel Hoskins after our very
full talk over the whole business, his account of his controversies
with King Ibn Sa'ud had not in the least shaken my conviction - a
conviction on which I was prepared to stake my whole reputation,
which was all that I had to stake as I had already sacrificed my

career by my fight for Arab independence - that, had he gone out to Arabia with President Roosevelt's first offer, made on behalf of the American and British Governments, on the lines of "the plan" that offer would have been accepted. I could only draw the rather disappointing conclusion that the British and American Governments are not prepared to make the relatively light sacrifices involved in "the plan" even to save the Jews from persecution, torture and death. If, however, I am wrong on this point the opportunity presents itself for putting the matter to the test. If the two Governments are really desirous of an arrangement on the lines of "the plan" and are prepared to make to Ibn Sa'ud a firm offer in that sense I am convinced that the King will accept it - but it must be a firm offer on the lines of "the plan" to be accepted or rejected as it stands without modification or bargaining. If, on the other hand, the two Governments do not want to make the sacrifices involved and are at the same time satisfied that Colonel Hoskins' interpretation of Ibn Sa'ud's attitude is correct, let them at least make a gesture of goodwill to the Jews and confront Ibn Sa'ud with a firm offer (on the lines of "the plan") which he will, as they are advised, turn down. I have only my own conviction to pit against the views of Colonel Hoskins, but no harm can come of putting the matter to the test. Either "the plan" is accepted or the status quo remains intact without prejudice to anybody. For my part I guarantee (for what my guarantee is worth) that the suggested firm offer will be accepted if made by any reasonably intelligent person of indisputable goodwill * on behalf of the two Governments concerned. It is for those Governments now to show the genuineness of the goodwill they are so fond of proclaiming towards the Arabs and the Jews.

H. St. J. PHILBY,

17.11.1943."

---

* omission

** substitution: 1.   "would not permit my return,"

2.   "statement, made by Colonel Hoskins to Dr. Weizmann (but not repeated to me) was that Colonel Hoskins started by asking the King whether he would see Dr. Weizmann; that the King replied that he would consider the matter but some days elapsed without his returning to the subject. Concluding from this that the answer was negative, Colonel Hoskins asked him whether he would meet one of Dr. Weizmann's colleagues? It was then that the King is reported to have broken out against Dr. Weizmann, and the Scheme. Colonel Hoskins"

3.   "since"

Sources: St. John Philby's papers, St. Anthony's College, Oxford Box X, File 3.
F.O. 371/40139 X/P 0976 E206/206/31 Dated 5 Jan. 1944.

Appendix P: Saudi Arabi Today

Source: Fouad Al-Farsy.   _Saudi Arabia_.   London: Stacey International, 1980.

Bibliography

I. Primary Sources

Ben-Gurion, David. Letter to H. St. John Philby. Esq., C.I.E. Dated 31 May 1937. The Central Zionist Archieves, Jerusalem. File S25/10095.

Great Britain. Foreign Office. Series 371 and Volumes: 13010, 16878, 20805, 23245, 24587, 24588, 24589, 27270, 27278, 34975, 34976, 35035, 35036, 35038, 40129, 40139.

_____. Parliamentary Papers. Command: Palestine Royal Commission Report, Cmd. 5479, 1937. Peel Report.

Palestine. Statement of Policy by His Majesty's Government in the United Kingdom, Cmd. 5513, 1937. White Paper on Partition.

Palestine Partition Commission Report, Cmd. 5854, 1938. The Woodhead Report.

Correspondence between Sir Henry McMahon and the Sherif Hussein of Mecca, July 1915-March 1916, Cmd. 5957 (Miscellaneous No. 3), 1939.

Hurewitz, J. C., ed. Diplomacy in the Near and Middle East. A Documentary Record: 1914-1956., Vol. II. New York: D. Van Nostrand Co., Inc., 1956.

Philby, H. St. John. Papers. St. Anthony's College, Oxford. Box X, File 3.

United States. Department of State. Foreign Relations of the United States, 1937, III (1954).

_____. Foreign Relations of the United States, 1939, IV (1955).

_____. Foreign Relations of the United States, 1940, III (1958).

_____. Foreign Relations of the United States, 1941, III (1959).

_____. Foreign Relations of the United States, 1942, IV (1963).

_____. Foreign Relations of the United States, 1943, IV (1964).

_____. Foreign Relations of the United States, 1944, V (1965).

II. Books

Amnstrong, H. C. Lord of Arabia. Beirut: Khayats, 1966.

Begin, Menachem. The Revolt: Story of the Irgun. New York: Schuman, 1951.

Brockelmann, Carl. History of the Islamic Peoples. New York: Capricorn, 1939.

Bryson, Thomas A. Seeds of Mideast Crisis. Jefferson, N.C.: McFarland 1981.

Ben-Gurion, David. Letters to Paula. Pittsburg: University of Pittsburg Press, 1972.

_____. My Talks With Arab Leaders. Jerusalem: Keter Books, 1972.

Bullard, Sir Reader. The Camels Must Go: An Autobiography. London: Faber and Faber, 1961.

Campbell, Thomas M.. ed. The Diaries of Edward R. Stettinius, Jr. 1943-1946. New York: New Viewpoint, 1975.

Cattan, Henry. Palestine, The Arabs and Israel. London: Longman, 1969.

Churchill, Winston. Triumph and Tragedy., Vol. 6. Boston: Mifflin, 1953.

_____. Memoirs of the Second World War. New York: Bonanza, 1978.

Esco Foundation for Palestine Inc. Palestine: A Study of Jewish, Arab, and British Policies, 2 Vol, New Haven: Yale University Press, 1947.

Forbes, Rosita. Conflict, Angora to Afghanistan. New York: Frederick A. Stokes, 1931.

Garnett, David, ed. The Letters of T. E. Lawrence. London: Cape, 1938.

Glubb, Sir John Bagot. A Soldier with the Arabs. London: Hodder and Stoughton, 1957.

Goitein, S. D. Jews and Arabs: Their Conflicts Through the Ages. New York: Schoken, 1970.

Goralski, Robert. World War II Almanac: 1935-1945 A Political and Military Record. New York: Putnam, 1981.

Graves, Philip. Palestine, The Land of Three Faiths. Westport, Connecticut: Hyperion, 1976.

Helms, Christine. The Cohesion of Saudi Arabia. Baltimore: John Hopkins University Presss, 1981.

Hitti, Philip K. Islam. A Way of Life. Minneapolis: University of Minnesota Press, 1970.

Holt, P. M., ed. The Cambridge History of Islam. Vol. 1. London: Cambridge University Press, 1970.

Howarth, David. The Desert King: A Life of Ibn Saud. London: Collins, 1964.

Hull, Cordell. The Memoirs of Cordell Hull. Vol. II. New York: MacMillan, 1948.

Hurewitz, J. C. The Struggle for Palestine. New York: Greenwood Press, 1968.

Jabotinsky, V. The Jewish War Front. London: 1940.

Kedourie, Elie. In the Anglo-Arab Labyrinth: The McMahon-Husayn Correspondence and Its Interpretations 1914-1939. London: Cambridge University Press, 1976.

Kennedy, Sir Alexander B. W. Petra: Its History and Monuments. London: Country Life, 1925.

Kirk, George. "The Middle East in the War", Survey of International Affairs. London: Oxford University Press, 1953.

Lenczowski, George. The Middle East in World Affairs. 4th Ed. Ithaca: Cornell University Press, 1980.

Loewenheim, Frances, ed. Roosevelt and Churchill: Their Secret Wartime Correspondence. New York: Saturday Review Press, 1975.

Lorimer, J. G. Gazetter of the Persian Gulf, Oman and Central Arabia. Shannon, Ireland: Irish Unversity Press, 1970.

Louis, William Roger. Imperialism At Bay. New York: Oxford University Press, 1978.

Marlow, John. Rebellion in Palestine. London: The Cresset Press, 1946.

Monroe, Elizabeth. Philby of Arabia. London: Faber and Faber Ltd., 1973.

Mousa, Suleiman. T. E. Lawrence: An Arab View. London: Oxford University Press, 1966.

Nyrop, Richard F, ed. Area Handbook for Saudi Arabia. Washington, D.C.: American University Foreign Area Studies, 1977.

Parks, James. A History of Palestine from 135 A.D. to Modern Times. New York: Oxford University Press, 1949.

_____. Whose Land? A History of the Peoples of Palestine. New York: Taplinger, 1971.

Peake, Pasha (Lt. Col. Fredrick G. Peake C.B.E.). A History of Jordan and its Tribes. Coral Gables, Florida: University of Miami, 1958.

Pawle, Gerald. The War and Colonel Warden. New York: Alfred A. Knauph, 1963.

Philby, H. St. John. The Heart of Arabia. 2 Vols. London: Constable 1922.

_____. Arabia of the Wahhabis. Totowa, New Jersey: Cass, 1977. Reprint of London: Constable, 1928.

_____. The Empty Quarter. New York: Holt, 1933.

_____. Harum Al Rashid. New York: Appelton, 1934.

_____. Arabian Days. An Autobiography. London: Hale, 1948.

_____. Arabian Highlands. Ithaca, New York: Cornell University Press, 1952.

_____. Arabian Jubilee. New York: John Day, 1953.

_____. Saudia Arabia. New York: Praeger, 1955.

_____. Arabian Oil Ventures (posthumonsly). Washington, D.C.: The Middle East Institute, 1964.

Rabinowicz, Oskar K. Fifty Years of Zionism. A Historical Analysis of Dr. Weizmann's 'Trial and Error'. London: Robert Anscombe & Co., 1952.

Rentz, Geroge. "The Wahhabis." In Vol. 1, Religion in the Middle East: Three Religions in Concord and Conflict, 2 Vols. ed., A. J. Arberry. London: Cambridge University Press, 1969.

Rihani, Ameen. Ibn Sa'oud of Arabia: Maker of Modern Arabia. Boston: Mifflin, 1928.

Rubin, Barry M. The Arab States and the Palestine Conflict. Syracuse: Syracuse University Press, 1981.

Samuel, The Rt. Hon. Viscount. Memoirs. London: The Cresset Press, 1945.

Sanger, Richard H. The Arabian Peninsula. Freeport, New York: Cornell University Press, 1954.

Stettinins, Edward R. Jr. Roosevelt and the Russians: The Yalta Conference. Garden City: Doubleday Co., 1949.

Storrs, Ronald. Orientations. London: Ivor Nicholson & Watson, 1937.

Troeller, Gary. The Birth of Saudi Arabia: Britain and the Rise of the House of Sa'ud. London: Cass, 1976.

Twitchell, Karl S. Saudi Arabia. Princeton: Princeton University Press, 1947.

Van Der Meulen, David. The Wells of Ibn Saud. New York: Praeger, 1957.

Weisal, Meyer, ed. Chaim Weizmann: A Biography by Several Hands. New York: Atheneum, 1963.

Weizmann, Chaim. Trial and Error: The Autobiography of Chaim Weizmann. New York: Schoken, 1966. Reprint of London: Weizmann Foundation, 1949.

Williams, E. T., ed. Dictionary of National Biography 1951-1960. London: Oxford University Press, 1971.

Winder, R. Bayly. Saudi Arabia in the Nineteenth Century. London: MacMillian, 1965.

Zwemer, Rev. S. M. Arabia: The Cradle of Islam. New York: Fleming H. Revell Co., 1900.

III. Articles

Busch, Noel F. "The King of Arabia." Life, 31 May 1943, pp. 71-88.

Philby, H. St. John. "The Palestine Problem." Contemporary Review, Vol. 152, No. 861, September 1937, pp. 264-269.

_____ "The Arabs and the Future of Palestine." Foreign Affairs. October 1937, pp. 156-166.

_____. "King Ibn Saud Speaks At Last." Asia, December 1938, pp. 717-718.

_____. "The Land of Midian." The Middle East Journal, Vol. 9, No. 2, September 1955, pp. 116-129.

_____. "Saudi Arabia: The New Statute of the Council of Ministers." The Middle East Journal, 1958, pp. 318-323.

The New York Times. Articles used were:

"Palestine Arabs End Strike Today." October 12, 1936, p. 9.

"Ibn Saud is Evasive on Palestine Plan." July 14, 1937, p. 11.

"Proposal by Philby." January 16, 1938, p. 31.

"French Drop Plan for a Syrian King." August 7, 1939, p. 5.

"Zionist at White House." February 9, 1940, p. 8.